SKIN DEEP

A.J. DANIELS

DEDICATION

To my husband. I love you to infinity and beyond. Thank you for
supporting me in this adventure

To my dad. I miss you.

"Scars remind us where we've been, they don't have to dictate where we're going."
-    Agent David Rossi, *Criminal Minds*.

NOTE FROM THE AUTHOR

The author has taken creative liberties with all names, places, and organizations mentioned in this book, and are not a reflection of any person, living or dead, or organization.

SKIN DEEP is the first book in the Behind These Eyes series but each book in the series can be read as a standalone, although, it's recommended to read them in order

ACKNOWLEDGEMENTS

First and foremost, I'd like to thank my husband for standing behind me and encouraging me to pursue this dream. I love you, J.

LC, thank you for sticking by me and allowing me to throw random plot ideas and scenes at you. For being my *Criminal Minds* buddy, and for lending me your engagement story about catching crabs at the beach. Here's to another ten years, Bestie.

Taylor at Imagination Uncovered, you did an amazing job on this cover, and I can't wait to work with you again.

Eve Arroyo, my editor, thank you for taking on a newbie author. I look forward to working with you again in the future.

All my beta readers. You ladies are amazing and I'm thankful for each and every one of you.

To Team Titan, if it weren't for you ladies and gents I don't think I would've had the courage to pursue this writing thing. Thank you for your support and encouragement. ILYH. **#TitanStrong.**

To the readers who stuck with me and read *Skin Deep* from beginning to end, thank you for taking a chance on a new author. I hope you enjoyed the ride.

PROLOGUE

1996

Cold lifeless eyes that once mirrored his own stare back at him. The sweet rush of adrenaline still courses through his veins. It's a much better high than any he's experienced before. Even killing the damn cat didn't make him feel like this.

An evil smirk picks at the corner of his mouth as he pushes his sister's lifeless body into the pool. Now she won't steal his favourite toy truck. Now she won't bother him when he's trying to watch his favourite cartoons in the morning.

He forces a tear to run down his cheeks when he hears his parents running through the living room and out the screen door that separates the house from the backyard. His mom shrieks when she sees his sister floating face down. His dad frantically jumps in to try and save her.

But it's too late. He's had his first taste of killing something bigger than an animal and he can't wait to be able to experience the rush again.

CHAPTER ONE

2011

"Congratulations, baby," Parker's mother says giving him a hug.

"Thanks, Mom." Staring down at his newly printed degree he can't believe he actually did it. He managed to graduate with a Bachelor of Science Degree.

"Well done, son," his dad says, clapping a hand on his back.

"Thanks, Dad."

Looking around at all the graduates and the amount of happiness radiating from them he can't help but feel glad to finally be getting out of this place. If it were up to him he would've joined the Royal Canadian Mounted Police, RCMP, right after high school. But Jason, Mike, and he had made a pact when they were ten that they would all join at the same time. Then Jay enlisted in the military right after high school graduation and Mike decided to party his way through Europe. So he did the only thing he could do, he agreed to follow his parents' wishes and continue on with his education to get his Bachelor's degree.

But Mike had returned from Europe two years ago and Jay ended his four-year enlistment a year ago. Now Jay and Mike were waiting for him to finish his degree before the three of them went off to Regina for RCMP training.

"So, when do you start?" his dad inquires.

"In two months."

"Good."

Parker nods.

"Good, good," his dad says looking around while Parker checks his phone and his mother examines her nail beds. "Well, Lori. We should get going."

His mom smiles and gives him another hug before getting into their white Audi R8 Spyder.

His family is fucking loaded and his parents have no issues flaunting it with their expensive cars, elaborate parties, boats, and their houses. Yes, houses', as in more than one.

He never did see the need in having more than one fucking house.

"Call us when you get settled," his dad says as he sits down in the driver's seat.

"Yes, sir," he replies before his dad shuts the door and they're speeding off the next second.

When their tail lights disappear around the corner he feels like he can breathe again. He loves his family, he really does, but spending any lengthy amount of time with them is draining.

He needs a fucking drink after that encounter with his parents.

They still don't understand why he coaches at a football camp every summer or why his goal is to make it onto the RCMP's elite Emergency Response Team, ERT. The closest thing he could relate it to was a cross between the CIA and SWAT. His parents' didn't understand because he himself has over half a million dollars sitting in his bank account. Half a million which was about to become two million dollars after the inheritance from his grandparents kicks in in two months, on his twenty-third birthday.

He didn't have to work if he didn't want to and, truthfully, with all the studying he'd done during the school semester, he's grateful for that but he'd rather earn everything he wants than have it handed to him.

He shoots of several text messages before making his way back to his condo.

Parker: Pizza. Beer. Football. My place. I recorded last night's game.

Jay: I'll bring the pizza.

Mike: Fuck yes! I've got the beer.

CHAPTER TWO

2014

You don't have to do this, Ashley, she tells herself. *Just walk out the door and go to Kat's. She'll help you disappear. All you have to do is walk out the door and tell her everything that's happened.*

But out of fear Ashley doesn't move from straddling Adam's lap. Fear that he'll never let her leave. Fear that if she did manage to leave he's track her down and drag her right back here.

His hand runs up her thigh while the other snakes around her neck, holding her in the perfect position for him to kiss her. Hard. Empty beer and whiskey bottles and half smoked joints litter the floor around the espresso colored coffee table of their living room.

This has become a nightly routine for them; they drink, get high, and fuck. Adam likes to remind her nightly of how much she needs him. How she'd have nothing if it weren't for him. She doesn't ever correct him because he's right. He's created such a void that her family and friends have refused to speak to her until she lets him go. Except Kat and Alice. They've been the only constant in her life.

She hasn't picked up a razor blade since they started seeing each other more frequently. Though, Adam, along with the drinking and pot, have become a replacement for the blade.

Adam slams back his shot of Jack Daniels and then the rest of his Coors Light before crushing his mouth to hers again. He tastes like whiskey and beer; it's a combination she's gotten used to over the last several months.

His grip tightens in her hair, almost painfully, pulling her head back, and exposing her neck to his roaming mouth. Adam's teeth nip at her jaw. She moans and arches closer to him, urging him to go lower. She needs to feel his mouth on her breasts, but he doesn't take the hint.

His hand continues roaming up her thigh and then circles around to squeeze her ass, bringing her body closer to his. She can feel his hard length against his zipper and suddenly she would do anything to have him inside of her. To live in the fantasy of the safety his arms would provide. But that's all it would be. A fantasy. Because nothing about him is safe. The hands roaming her body are just a part of his arsenal of weapons; used to break her down physically until she's compliant the way he wants. And the mouth trailing kisses along her collarbone and up her neck is the worst weapon of all; capable of making her feel like she deserves whatever punishment he deems fit. Right now, she tries to push that knowledge out of her mind because sex with him is the only way she knows how to cope with it all. The sex provides her with a high unlike any amount of pot would.

She grabs a fistful of his shaggy, brown hair and tries to force his mouth further down her body, but he doesn't move from his assault on her neck.

"Adam . . ." she breathes heavily.

"Tell me what you want, Ashley."

She runs her palm over the growing bulge in his jeans, but he pulls away shaking his head.

"Words, Ashley. I want to hear you say the words."

His hands and mouth go back to their roaming assault on her body, and she can't think straight. Doubt and guilt start to crawl their way back up her spine. Not ready to face reality, she tries to grab his hands and place them on her breasts, but it doesn't work.

She starts grinding against him, but he puts his hands on her hips and stills her movements. Frustration builds inside of her as the promise of the fantasy slowly crashes around her.

His phone rings from across the living room, and in his haste to answer it he tosses her on the other side of the couch.

"Who is it?" disappointment laces her voice.

It stops ringing before he can answer it but something on the screen has caught his attention because his fingers fly over the keyboard. "It's no one," he lies. "Look, babe, I gotta head out for a few hours." He pockets his phone, rearranges himself, and reaches for his suit jacket. "I'll call you later," he throws over his shoulder before closing the front door of the apartment behind him.

"Yeah, sure," she whispers into the quiet. Her body starts to shake in anger and disappointment. She was about to overlook all of Adam's abusive and controlling ways again, just for another taste of a fantasy she knew she could never have. Silent tears roll down her cheeks as her thumb traces the fading scars on her inner wrist.

Her phone pings with a new message, bringing her out of her daze.

Kat: Bellinis and chocolate cake?
Ashley: Heck yes! At Joey's?

Kat: Already here.

She laughs at Kat's message. It's possibly the first time she's laughed in over a week. Maybe she doesn't need Adam to keep her distracted from the darkness tonight. Maybe drinks and chocolate cake with one of her best friends will be able to do the job Adam couldn't.

12 years ago

She hates this place. She hates the cold, the snow, and the stuck-up kids she's forced to go to school with. She hates not being able to see her cousin and best friend whenever she wants. It's been two years since they emigrated from Cape Town, South Africa to Toronto, Canada. Six months after moving here and starting school, she forced herself to get rid of her slightly British accent. Even then, at twelve years old, she couldn't stand being laughed at every time she opened her mouth. She hated it. She wanted to cry and she wanted to go home. Not the house they lived in here, but back home to the country she knows and loves.

But what she didn't miss was feeling like she was a worthless use of space. Yeah, families are awesome like that, not! Don't get her wrong, her parents, her cousins, and some of her aunts and uncles are great, but others not so much, especially her grandmother on her dad's side. For Ashley's whole life she always felt like she and her brother, Chris, were never good enough and could never live up to her grandmother's standards. Even as a little girl; walking into her home and seeing pictures of all her cousins on her walls but almost none of her and Chris made her feel like they weren't wanted. Oh, there would be, but it was only a small 2x2 image of them tucked away into the corner of a frame that already held a big picture of their cousins.

Some might think it weird how close her family and extended family were when she was growing up in South Africa, but that's how life was over there. They saw aunts, uncles, and cousins every weekend and sometimes during the week too. In the summer, they saw each other several times a week. She always wondered why her grandmother never loved them like the other cousins. What was so wrong with them? Were they that unlovable? Was she ashamed of her family?

The restaurant is dimly lit and loud cheers sail up from the bar area as the Vikings score another touchdown against the Titans. The hostess leads her to a booth in the dining room where Kat is studying the menu. Her long, brunette hair isn't up in its usual messy bun tonight. Instead, it's cascading in waves down her back. She's so focused on the menu Kat doesn't look up when Ashley slides into the opposite side of the booth.

"What's up?"

Kat's head snaps up, and her amber eyes narrow. "They changed the menu."

"What? Please tell me they didn't get rid of the chocolate lava cake. I was promised chocolate tonight." She reaches over to grab the menu out of Kat's hands. She breathes a sigh of relief when her eyes scan down the menu and find chocolate lava cake listed as the first dessert mentioned.

"They didn't, but they did remove the lettuce wraps." Kat pouts in disappointment that her favourite item was no longer being offered.

Ashley's eyes widen in horror when the realization she never grabbed her jacket before leaving the apartment catches up with her as she hands Kat back her menu. The bruises on both of her arms are fully exposed. Her wrist and scars thankfully covered by the oversized bangle she chose to wear today.

Kat grabs both of her arms and turns them over, exposing the black and blue marks. "Ash?"

"It's nothing, Kat." She pulls her arms away and tried to hide them under the table.

"It's nothing?" Kat repeats, not understanding.

When she doesn't answer, Kat huffs and opens her mouth to say something just as their waitress comes to take their order. Kat orders the chili chicken, and she orders the chocolate lave cake. Both of them ordering peach bellinis.

When their waitress leaves Kat levels her with a knowing look. "Did he do this?"

"Who?"

She tries to act dumb, but it's not working. They both know there is only one "he" in her life.

Adam wasn't violent when they first started dating. In fact, it was only supposed to be a casual thing. A way for her to chase the high she so desperately craved and Adam, well . . . Adam got laid.

But then he started getting possessive, saying he couldn't stand the thought of her with other men. So, they began only seeing each other, at least that's what she thought. It turns out Adam had other ideas.

She knew there was at least one other woman for sure, but who knows how many there were. The first time she confronted him about it was almost a year ago to date.

"Who is she, Adam?"

"What are you talking about," he continues flipping through the TV channels, ignoring her.

She throws the lipstick-stained shirt down on his lap, "The woman whose lipstick is on your collar."

"I'm warning you, Ashley. Let it go," he demands, lowering his feet from the coffee table to the carpet.

"No, I won't let it go, Adam. Who is she?"

Adam pushes up off the couches and stalks towards her. "I said let it go."

"Fuck you!" she throws back.

She didn't see the first slap coming but she'll never forget the sound it made when his palm hit her cheek. It was like the first clap of thunder before a rain storm. It was so hard it threw her head back, and she stumbled until she hit the wall behind her.

Adam said she was imagining things, even after being confronted with the lipstick stain on his shirt. He said if she really believed that there was another woman then she was as stupid as she looked. After his rant, he summed it all up with, *"And what if I was seeing someone else? You need me more than I need you."*

"Are you? Adam, are you seeing someone else?"

"Jesus fucking Christ, Ashley!" Adam's voice gets louder with each sentence. *"You really think I have enough time to fuck someone else? What am I? Fucking Superman? I work my ass off to provide for you and this is the thanks I get?"*

When he'd finished yelling he stormed out of the apartment, coming back several hours later smelling like bourbon, saying how sorry he was.

He didn't know what'd happened and he swore he'd never hit her again. He said he loved her, and she believed him. Every second day since has been a repeat of that night; he would come home smelling like bourbon and another woman's perfume. She would ask him about it or refuse to sleep with him, and he would *discipline* her with his fists. It was an ugly reminder of just how far she'd go to keep the emotional pain at bay. Every hit, every kick was just another reminder of how weak she was.

"Adam," Kat says in frustration, bringing her back to reality, "Did Adam do that?"

"No, he didn't. I fell down some stairs at the university." She winces internally at her lame excuse for a lie.

"I call bullshit, Ashley."

"What do you want, Kat? You want me to say I screwed up? That I screwed up so badly I made him hit me?"

"Ash, you didn't make him hit you!" Kat raises her voice.

"Yes, I did. I accused him of cheating again, and he got so mad he went to the bar and drank bourbon until two a.m. When he came home I wouldn't stop with all the questions. I know how he is when he drinks." She raises her voice too. "I fucking knew! But I still made him angry. I deserved it." She looks around the nearly empty restaurant, and her shoulders sink in relief when nobody turns around to stare.

"Jesus, Ashley, do you know how ridiculous that sounds? First, he makes you feel guilty when you want to hang out with your family and friends so you stopped coming out. You don't even talk to your mom anymore, Ashley. You two used to be so close." Sadness invades Kat's eyes. "Then he insists you shouldn't drive to campus by yourself. Now he drops you off and picks you up. That's if you even make it to campus. You can't even go out without him. Honestly, I'm surprised he isn't here right now."

"Kat—"

"The only thing you're allowed to do is work at the library, and God knows what he's doing while you're at work. And now this?" Kat falls back against the booth, all the while keeping her eyes focused on hers. "It's got to stop, Ash. You have to leave." She sighs.

Ashley shakes her head. "I can't leave."

"Why not?"

"I deserved what he did, and if I did leave he would just track me down and bring me back. He's told me before that if I try to leave he'll make sure I never do it again."

"My roommate's moving out this week, and I haven't been able to find anyone to replace her yet. You could move into my apartment. It's a secure building, you need a code to get in." Kat leans forward and takes one of Ashley's hands in hers. "You do not deserve this. Don't think for a second you do, okay?"

"Okay," she whispers.

"Good, so you'll move into my place this week."

"No, Kat. I can't leave him. He'll find me." Her eyes burn with unshed tears, but she tries her damnedest to hold them back. She knows she can survive this. All she has to do is keep Adam happy enough so he won't hit her again.

"Okay, Alice and I sort of came up with a plan in case this ever happened." Kat sighs in defeat, letting go of Ashley's hand. "Don't be mad."

"What plan?"

"If at any point you decide enough is enough, no matter what time is it, you send us a group message asking to meet you at our spot."

"Our spot? The park?"

Kat nods, "We'll both be there by the time you arrive and we'll get you out of town. Adam will never know where you went."

"Thank you."

"You don't have to thank us. We're your best friends, Ash. We just can't stand the thought of what that monster's doing to you."

Ashley changes the subject and the two of them finish their second round of bellinis before Kat drops her off at the apartment she shares with Adam.

At three a.m., she scrambles out of bed when she hears glass bottles crashing to the floor and a loud curse. Her stomach sinks with the realization that Adam might've been with that woman, in her bed, when he should've been here in their bed.

As soon as she pulls open the bedroom door her nose crinkles at the familiar smell of another woman's perfume mixed with the sour stench of bourbon.

"Adam?" she calls into the dark.

"What the fuck do you want?" he spits out from the dining room.

"Where were you?" She turns to the wall by her side and flips on the light switch.

The sight of Adam should shock her when she turns back to face him but, sadly, it doesn't. He's leaning over the dining room table and the vase that once stood tall on the table holding a dozen long-stemmed, red roses is now laying in shattered pieces on the hardwood floor.

His hair is a mess, his clothes are wrinkled, and his shirt is buttoned up all wrong.

"Out."

"Out? Out where?" She's playing with fire right now.

"Jesus Christ, Ashley!" He stands up, swiping his arm across the top of table, sending a number beer bottles crashing to the floor, joining the vase.

Adam stalks toward her until they're standing toe to toe, and she can feel his breath against her cheek. "It's none of your fucking business where I've been," he growls.

She tries to take a step back, but he grabs around her neck and pulls her against him so their bodies are flush. "Now, are we going to finish where we left off this afternoon?"

She tries to push against his chest but it's like pushing against a brick wall, "No."

"No?" he hisses in her face, tightening his grip around her neck. "You don't ever say no to me, Ashley. I'm all you have, bitch."

"I'm not sleeping with you while you smell like another woman, Adam."

Adam's grip loosens momentarily in shock, but she takes the opportunity to get out of his grasp. He doesn't let her get very far before he grips her arms and swings her around, slamming her back into the wall. His fist connects with her jaw and then with her stomach. She doubles over in pain and sinks down to the floor, curling up in the fetal position while his boot lands kick after kick to her ribs. He doesn't stop until she passes out from the pain.

CHAPTER THREE

Ashley wakes up in a hospital bed with no memory of how she ended up there or how long she'd been there. All she knows is that she's alone and she fucking hurt. It feels like a crushing weight is sitting on her ribs.

"Hey, you're awake." Kat slips in through the open door and sits down in the vacant chair next to her hospital bed.

"How long have I been here?"

"Only since yesterday," Kat answers.

All she can is nod her head because she's still confused as to how she ended up here. The last memory she has is lying on the dining room floor of the apartment she shared with Adam while he continued to kick her. Surely, he wouldn't have called the ambulance, would he?

"I found you," Kat answers her unspoken questions

"You?" Her voice is strained from not having used it in what feels like years.

Kat hands her a glass of water from the pitcher next to the bed, "You weren't answering your cell, and after what I saw that night I got worried. I still have a key from before he moved in so I used it to get in and found you on the floor." Her voice hitches as she tries to hold back a sob.

"It was bad, Ash. Your body was so contorted; I was barely able to make you out laying on the floor. I couldn't tell if you were breathing or not, and the 9-1-1 operator told me not to move you. You scared me half to death."

Tears flow freely from Ashley's green eyes. "I'm so sorry, Kat."

"Shh," Kat soothes. "You have nothing to be sorry about. I'm just glad I found you when I did." Kat leans over and throws her one arm around her but pulls back when Ashley winces in pain. "Shit, sorry. I forgot you have a couple cracked ribs. They had to tape them. You'll need to take it easy for the next several weeks."

"Adam?"

"He wasn't there when I found you." Kat avoids eye contact and starts fiddling with the sleeves of her sweater. "He hasn't come by the hospital either."

Kat doesn't get restless and she sure as heck doesn't fiddle with anything so Ashley knows whatever Kat is trying to hide can't be good.

"Just tell me. Please, Kat. I can handle it."

Kat looks doubtful but takes a moment to take a deep breath before dropping the bomb. "Adam's engaged."

She laughs but when she turns to Kat and notices the serious look on her face, her smile fades, "What?"

"I'm sorry, Ash. It was in the paper this morning. Apparently, she's from a family of very renowned lawyers. The firm is number one in the city. The article said Adam and their daughter have been dating for the last year. It said he proposed yesterday. Right around the same time we were at Joey's. That's why I was calling you."

"He came home at three a.m. smelling like bourbon and some woman's perfume," Ashley whispers, not willing to believe that Adam would propose to another woman while he was with her.

The knowledge that Adam not only cheated but got engaged to another woman should upset her at the very least but it doesn't. She doesn't feel anything at all.

"I'm sorry, Ash."

"Are you?" she questions.

Kat sighs. "No, I'm not sorry you're finally rid of him. But, I am sorry he did this to you. I'm sorry I didn't try and get you out of there sooner."

She closes her eyes, praying sleep will claim her quickly. Somehow, deep down, she knows this won't the last time she hears of Adam. This is just the beginning.

It has been two weeks since she was released from the hospital, and she hasn't left her apartment since Kat dropped her off.

She's so tired. Tired of pretending she's okay. Tired of pretending there isn't a black hole inside of her. It feels like a weight pressing on her chest, and she can't breathe.

She wants the darkness to take her away so she doesn't have to fight the constant battle of pursuing a physical pain that would distract her from the emotional one she fights to keep at bay. She doesn't want to struggle anymore.

She doesn't give a shit about anything anymore, not her job and not the classes she hasn't been to in two weeks. If she's hungry, which is very rare, she orders from the pizza place down the street. She keeps the apartment in total darkness, glad she'd purchased the blackout curtains.

She doesn't know what day it is anymore. The minute she'd gotten home she turned off her phone and hasn't cracked open her laptop or turned on the TV since. She doesn't know if she can handle seeing all the notifications pop up about Adam's engagement. She had only just glanced at a picture of his fiancée when checking her Facebook in the hospital.

She's fucking perfect; blonde, blue-eyed, probably a size two, and her parents are rich. She's the exact opposite of Ashley's size twelve, curvy frame.

She's reluctant to call herself depressed but maybe she is. Adam was her drug of choice when the alcohol and pot didn't cut it, and she was fucking addicted.

She doesn't care about the rest; the controlling, the beatings, none of it, because she's addicted to the way he made the darkness in her fade away, if only for a few hours. But now she just feels lost.

She doesn't want to be in the apartment because it reminds her too much of him. But she has nowhere to go. If she allows herself to move in with Kat she'd have to constantly put on a brave face and pretend she was okay.

The person she is when she's alone and when she's among her friends are two very different people. When she's with them it seems like she's outgoing, like nothing could faze her. But when she's alone she retreats into a very dark place inside of herself.

She wants to keep her friends from having to see that other side of her. She doesn't want her two best friends to see her like that. To know just how broken she really is. Maybe she should've cared about the abuse, any sane person would, but to her it was just another reminder of how worthless she is.

She's suddenly very glad she'd taken Kat's key back when she'd realized she didn't have hers. She's grateful Kat wouldn't be walking in on her while she's at her lowest; when beer and whiskey bottles litter the floors of her apartment, when it smells like stale pot and new scars adorn her thighs and arms.

She started getting creative with her cuts after the first week of being home. Now instead of the neat, little lines, the words FAILURE and WORTHLESS decorate the tops of her thighs.

She couldn't stop and she hates herself for it. She doesn't

want to end her life; the cuts are never deep enough for it to get that far. She just wants to feel the physical pain so the emotional pain will take a backseat and leave her alone. The physical pain never stays long enough, though, and soon the emotions come flooding right back in again.

She wants to stop cutting, God does she ever want to stop, but she needs it. It's the one thing she has that will make it all feel better. It's the one thing she knows she will always have because it won't leave. It won't make her empty promises and then abandon her when she really needs it. It takes all her pain away, just like it promised. It won't tell her it loves her and then break her heart, and it most assuredly won't call her worthless.

It will always be there for her, and she needs it.

She knows there are drugs out there that will have the same effect but she isn't stupid. She doesn't want to owe her life to the drugs. Even though, that's what she's currently doing; she owes her life to cutting, drinking, and pot. But it's different than heroin or cocaine.

It *is* different. Maybe if she keeps repeating it, one day it will be true.

She knows she also needs help because there's a chance the next time she grabs a blade she won't stop and that might be the one that ends her life. She can't bear to see the hurt and disappointment in her best friends' eyes but looking around her dark apartment, she knows she needs help tonight because if she doesn't get it, there may not be a tomorrow for her.

With a shaky breath and tears streaming down her cheeks, she stumbles to the kitchen in a drunken haze, finds her phone and dials, praying they'll forgive her and will help her get through this.

She's already decided she doesn't want to be admitted to the psych ward at the hospital. She wants to do this on her own with her two best friends. It's bad enough she'd have to see the pity in their eyes, she doesn't want to have to see it in the eyes of the doctors and nurses too. Was that selfish of her to put this on Kat and Alice? Maybe. But this was the only way she could see herself getting better.

Kat answers on the second rings, "Hello?"

"Kat—" Shit, she was slurring.

"Ash? What's wrong?"

"Need help. Can't make it stop." She hopes Kat can make out

her words because they don't sound right to her ears.

"Can't make what stop, Hun?"

Huh? Okay well she guesses her words are making sense.

"Soo drunk," she sings, then starts giggling. Her brow furrows as she tries to string together another sentence.

She has no idea what Kat says after that because her eyes started feeling heavy, and she passes out in the middle of her kitchen floor.

CHAPTER FOUR

Ashley wakes up in her bathtub with a bucket of ice being thrown on her.

"Nice of you to join us." Alice smiles, tucking the bucket under arms.

"What the hell, Alice?" she shrieks crossing her arms over her chest, trying to protect her body against the shivers that are threatening.

Alice shrugs, "Fastest way to sober you up. Get showered and come out to the living room. Kat and I'll clean up your apartment."

"I hate you." She glares at Alice's retreating back, but Alice doesn't miss a step as she flips her the bird over her shoulder and continues out to the living room.

These girls are her only family here. They're the ones who keep her sane without even realizing they're doing it. If it weren't for them she probably wouldn't have made it this far.

After removing her clothes, she looks down at the scars decorating her wrists and thighs, and knows it's true. Without those ladies she would've taken the blade deeper a long time ago. The irony is they still have no idea about her secret.

That's about to change. Tonight. She's going to tell them everything. She hopes Kat and Alice will still accept her afterwards.

Turning the water off and stepping out of the tub she wraps the oversized bath towel around her body and goes in search of a hair brush in the clutter that's taken over the bathroom counter. Most of the stuff is Adam's.

He hated when she wore makeup, so she'd stopped. She got tired of always hearing comments like, "You don't need to wear that shit. Who are you trying to attract?" And her personal favorite, "You look like a whore with all that shit on your face. Take it off."

Yeah, the guy's an asshole.

After her hair is void of all knots, she grabs a pair of black yoga pants and a tank top from her dresser drawers. She gets dressed and takes a deep breath, preparing herself to go in search of her best friends.

"You guys didn't need to do this." Ashley gestures to the spotless living room, dining room, and kitchen.

There's not one beer or whiskey bottle in sight, and all the pizza delivery boxes are broken down and piled up by the door.

"We'll take those down with us when we leave." Kat nods towards the recycling then moves towards Ashley and engulfs her in a hug.

"Thanks, guys." She wraps her arms around Kat.

"So, spill." Alice drops herself onto the L-shaped couch. She was never one to beat around the bush. Alice cringes every time someone tries to make small talk with her, preferring deep meaningful conversations instead.

With a sigh, Ash sits down next to Alice, folding her legs under her, while Kat takes up the seat on the other side of Ash. There's no easy way to do this so Ash slowly turns over her wrists, and tears instantly leak out of her eyes. This was why she chose not to wear her usual sweater over her tank top.

"I can't stop."

"Jesus, Ash." Alice grabs the wrist closest to her and gently runs her fingers over the multiple red and angry scars.

"How long?" Kat asks quietly.

"Since I was fourteen."

Eleven years.

"Why?"

Ashley shrugs and turns her head to Kat. "I was bullied a lot because of my accent and where I was from. I didn't make friends easily and when it turned out I was way ahead of my grade the bullying became worse. I couldn't cope and my parents and teachers wouldn't listen. At first I turned to sex and lost my virginity to the first guy to ever show interest in me." She takes a deep breath before continuing, "I thought he was my best friend. I thought I could trust him. That he would be there when I needed him, but . . ."

"But?" Alice prods.

"But all I was to him was a quick fuck. Someone he called when he needed to get off, but during the week at school he acted like I didn't exist. Then he started joining in on the bullying. My parents never allowed us to stay home from school unless we were really sick, so I had to endure it every day; until one day I couldn't stand the emotional pain anymore."

Ashley absently runs her fingers over the scars leading up her inner arm. "I guess my dad had forgotten to put his razor and blades away after a shower one morning. So, when it was my turn to shower, I saw them. It helped for a while, and I did everything I could to lose the accent and dumb myself down. The bullying eventually stopped just before my junior year."

"Ash." Kat grabs Ashley's hand and squeezes it reassuringly, but pain is evident in her eyes when she looks up.

"In a weird way, Adam helped. When I was with him I didn't have to think about cutting. We were always drinking, getting high, or fucking."

Kat and Alice both snort next to her.

"What? It's true. I know it's not what either of you want to hear, but it was like I replaced one addiction with another. Except for the abuse."

"He hit you, Ash. Repeatedly," Kat adds.

"I know, and I know you wanted me to leave him, Kat. But I loved him. I know it probably doesn't make any sense, but in a way, I was using him too. When I woke up in the hospital that day and you told me about him getting engaged, I should've felt something, anything. I mean, we were together for just over a year. I should've felt something but I didn't."

"What do you mean you didn't feel anything?" Alice asks

"I mean I didn't feel a thing. I was just numb. It's like I stopped giving a shit. When I left the hospital I still felt numb. That's why I got hammered and kept getting hammered every day for almost two weeks. At least when I was drunk I had an excuse as to why I wasn't feeling anything. When the alcohol started fading away I'd drink just enough to get drunk again. Eventually that stopped working. That's when I found Adam's blades."

"How bad, Ash?" Alice asks

"Bad." Ashley turns to look at her, noticing for the first time the tears brimming her eyes.

Kat sighs on the other side of Ashley and wraps one arm around her shoulders the other around her chest, "So what do you need us to do?"

"Honestly? You're doing it right now. I just need to know you girls will be there. No matter what."

"We're not going anywhere, Ash," Alice announces.

"Can I suggest something, though?" Kat chimes in.

"What's that?"

"We'll get to your living arrangements soon but for now how about we get rid of everything in this apartment that reminds you of that jackass—and the blades."

"Sounds like a plan." Ashley smiles for the first time in two weeks.

Ashley, Kat, and Alice work until the early hours of the morning collecting and packing everything that belongs to Adam or that reminds Ashley of him.

She's surprisingly relaxed when she finally falls into bed. But, she's not asleep for fifteen minutes when she hears the front door squeak open followed by a crash of boxes.

Thinking it's one of the girls, Ashley throws off the blankets and makes it half way to her bedroom door before a very familiar voice travels in from the living room. A very familiar, *male* voice.

"What are you doing here, Adam? I wasn't expecting you to show your face again." Ashley leans against the doorjamb of her bedroom. She doesn't think she can stand up straight right now even if she wants to. Her ribs still fucking kill, but at least the bruising has faded a lot over the last week.

"I live here, babe," Adam slurs.

"No. No, you don't. You almost fucking killed me, Adam. And, per every media outlet in this town, you're engaged. Or did you just happen to forget that little tidbit of information?"

"I have no choice. I have to marry her if I ever want to make partner in the firm. But I came back to you, babe. I come home to you."

"You had a choice, Adam. There are plenty of other law firms where you could make partner without having to marry anyone. You had a choice and you chose wrong."

Folding her arms across her chest, she tries to stand up straighter and take a deep breath, but that just causes her ribs to protest in pain. But her voice comes out surprisingly strong. "You need to leave. Now."

Somehow, with her trying not to look like she's in pain, she doesn't notice Adam moving closer until he's standing directly in front of her.

"You don't get to walk away from me, Ashley. You don't get to end this until I say I'm done, and I'm not done with you yet." He grabs her by both arms and pushes her against the doorjamb. "Do you hear me?"

Blinding pain rockets across her ribs, making it difficult for her to breathe.

"Adam, you're hurting me," she cries.

"I don't want to, Ashley. But it seems to be the only way to get it through that stupid brain of yours."

Adam pulls her forward a couple inches before slamming her back against the wall.

"Adam, stop, please," she begs.

Adam's mouth is set in a hard line and his eyes burn with anger as his hands squeeze tighter around her arms, "You don't seem to get it, Ashley. You don't get to tell me what to do. You just get to shut up and be ready and waiting for me when I come home."

Her body finally starts listening to the commands her brain is sending, and her knee shoots up and connects with Adam's balls and momentarily stuns him.

She takes the opportunity to get away from him and runs back into the bedroom, hoping to lock herself in, away from Adam's advances, he manages to push the door open before she can shut it.

He only has a split second to react after chasing her into the bedroom before something wizzes by his head and hits the wall to his right.

She is standing on the opposite side of the room, fear emanating from every pore of her body. The fact that the lamp she just threw at Adam's head didn't hit its mark makes her more fearful. Adam's eyes go black as they lock onto his prey.

She twists around and grabs the picture frame before pulling back and hurling it at him, but he ducks and moves out the way just in time. The glass shatters as it hits the wall, and shards fly in all directions, with some hitting his back, but he doesn't flinch.

His nostrils flare as he stalks toward her and tackles her to the floor, pining both of her arms above her head, with one hand holding her wrists, and straddling her legs.

She screams as she tries to twist her wrists out of his grasp, but Adam tightens his hold. She tries to bring her knees up again, but Adam has successfully pinned them down.

"Fucking stop moving, Ashley."

Anger is rolling off him in waves as she continues to struggle under him. Adam backhands her but when she continues to scream he lands one punch to her face, and she quiets, her body quivering in fear.

His hand comes up and grabs her face, squeezing her cheeks. "Now, I'm fucking starving so you're going to go and make me something to eat like a good little bitch, and you're not to speak until I allow you to, or those cracked ribs will turn into broken bones. Understand?"

Her eyes round at the coldness of his voice.

Adam smirks. "You didn't think I'd check up on you, did you? After all, I had to make sure you didn't tell those doctors the truth about what happened." Adam sighs disappointedly. "Oh, I know you told those two bitches everything but I'm looking forward to taking care of them so they don't go squealing to the wrong people." His lips draw back in a snarl. "It'll be fun watching as they realize they're about to take their last breaths. Not being able to scream. Not being to move."

Adam lets go of her and moves back to the living room, "Don't forget my food, Ashley, and don't think about warning those friends of yours either. You'll regret it if you do."

After Adam ate and drank himself into unconsciousness— despite his warnings, Adam still put away a full bottle of whiskey— she immediately went to work. Quietly grabbing her backpack and throwing as many things as she could into it while trying her hardest to be quiet.

Ashley knew when he drank that much chances of him waking up before morning were slim to none but she didn't want to play with fire. She didn't want to chance waking the bear and have all hell break loose.

It wasn't just her life in danger now. Adam threatened the lives of her two best friends and that didn't fly with her. She may not care what happens to her but she would protect those women with her life.

After throwing the last of her clothing into the backpack, she tiptoes passed Adam snoring on the couch, avoiding all the floorboards she knows creak.

Holding her breath, her hands shake when she quietly turns the lock in the front door and pries it open. She lets out her breath when Adam doesn't move on the couch.

As soon as the door closes behind her, her feet take off as fast as they can carry her down the two flights of stairs to the lobby and out the glass-paned doors. She sends off a quick message to Kat and Alice then ditches her phone in the nearest garbage can.

Ashley: Adam came back to the apartment. Long story. Meet at our spot in 30.

Adam knows her log-in information for her iCloud and he likes to use the "find my iPhone" app to keep track of her whereabouts. If what she has planned is going to have any chance of working, he can't know where she is. Which means, she'll be ditching a lot more than just her phone.

Kat and Alice are already waiting when she arrives at the park. Despite the streets light being on it's still dark outside so Kat and Alice don't see the new bruises and split lip until Ashley walks right up to them.

"Oh, my God, Ashley." Alice rushes towards her and immediately starts looking over the freshly colored black and blue skin.

"I'm fine."

"You're not fine, Ash," Kat points out.

"What happened?" Alice asks.

"What always happens. Except he took it too far this time. When he threatened both your lives something snapped, and I realized I couldn't stay there anymore."

"How'd you get out?"

Ashley scowls. "Adam never could turn down a good bottle of whiskey. He'll wake up with one hell of a hangover in the morning."

"What do you want to do now?" Kat inquires

Ashley looks from one woman to the other. "You said you guys had a plan." She stuffs one of her hands into the pocket of her capri pants and wraps the fingers of the other one around the strap of her backpack. "I think I'm ready to hear it now."

Kat and Alice share a look before turning back to Ashley. "Are you sure?" Kat asks.

Ashley sighs dropping and shaking her head. Her eyes squeeze shut against the tears threatening to spill. When she's confident she has control over the water works again she lifts her head and looks both women in the eyes, determination flashing in hers. "Yes. Adam's won too many times, but it ends now. I can't live like this anymore. I refuse to let the depression win again and if I stay here with Adam that's what will happen. And I refuse to let him make me his fuck buddy on the side."

"Okay," Alice acknowledges, motioning for them all to take a seat on each of the three swings. "Our plan, after meeting you here, was to get you out of town fast and without Adam being able to track you down. Right now, that means taking the greyhound bus to any destination you want. It doesn't have to be in Ontario."

"Alice and I have been putting some money aside from each of our paychecks every month for the last year. If this was to ever happen we wanted you to have a fast exit and not have to worry about expenses for a bit. We have about seven thousand dollars saved up."

Ashley eyes tear up again, "You guys didn't need to do that. That's a lot of money."

Alice shrugs. "We wanted to, and plus it's not all ours. Your family have been pitching in when they can as well."

"My family?"

Kat reaches over and slips her hand in Ashley's. "When your mom and dad and Chris couldn't get ahold of you they got worried and your dad called us. Alice and I told him what was happening and your dad went ballistic."

"He went down to Adam's law firm and confronted him. Your dad threatened to cut off his balls if he didn't leave you alone," Alice adds. "But because Adam is the monster he is, he had your dad arrested, claiming assault. Then he slapped him with a restraining order and added your name to it as well. Your dad isn't allowed within one-hundred feet of you and Adam. He isn't allowed any communication with you either. We set up the savings after that."

"That's ridiculous. Why didn't anyone at the firm stand up for my dad and say he never assaulted Adam?"

"It happened in the parking lot. Your dad caught him as he was coming back from lunch."

Realization dawns on Ashley while Alice speaks. "Adam came home with a black eye, about a year ago now I guess. He said one of the guys accidentally elbowed him when they were playing rugby after work. You mean he did it to himself?"

"It seems so. Your dad swears he never laid a hand on Adam, although he wanted to."

"You know, it should surprise me Adam would stoop so low to keep my family away from me, but it doesn't."

"Your dad just wanted you to be safe and away from that asshole. But Ash, if you decide to leave, you have to leave them behind too. This only works if you leave everyone here behind and become a whole new person," Alice warns.

"Well, everyone except for us," Kat adds with a small grin.

"Look, I don't expect you girls to pack up your lives and come with me."

Kat gave Alice another knowing look before both women turn to face her. Despite the warm, June night, she's shivering. The adrenaline from the events of the evening is finally leaving her body.

"We're coming with you," Alice states confidently.

She shakes her head, "No, your lives are here. You can't just pack up and move in one night."

Kat shakes her head, disputing Ashley's claim. "We can and we will. Nothing is holding us here. Our families aren't here, and we can switch our classes to distance ed. and complete them online."

"You need us more than we need to stay," Alice adds.

Ashley nods. "Any idea where you ladies would like to go?"

"I have a friend in BC. He could probably find us a condo down there," Alice supplies.

"All right." Ashley breathes a sigh of relief, and they plan to go back to Alice and Kat's apartments to grab some of their clothes before heading to the Greyhound bus depot.

It takes them three days to get from Ontario to BC on the bus. During that time, Ashley Martens ceased to exit, and Danielle Gilbert was born. Straight, shoulder-length, blonde hair became long, wavy, and black, reaching down to her lower back, thanks to extensions and a curling iron. She hates the idea of sticking her finger in her eye to put contacts in so her striking green eyes have to stay.

She looks into the mirror hanging in the women's bathroom of the bus stop but she doesn't recognize the person staring back at her.

"Hi, I'm Danielle," she says to herself in the mirror, faking a smile.

"Danielle. Danielle Gilbert." She tries out her new name again, but it feels funny on her tongue. "Well, it's now or never," she says to herself, taking a deep breath and pulling open the door to her new future, where Kat is now Nicole or Nic, and Alice is now Jessica or Jess.

CHAPTER FIVE

2015

"Nice shot," Jay says over his shoulder, reloading the next round into his Glock 17.

"Not too bad yourself," Parker fires back.

After he, Jay, and Mike completed their RCMP training in Regina, Saskatchewan four years ago, the three of them were assigned to the unit in Oceanview, British Columbia. Two years after joining all three of them were recruited to BC's Emergency Response Team. Now they were sergeants.

They fire off a couple more rounds before both their phones ring simultaneously.

"Collins," Parker answers.

"Miller," Jay answers.

Seconds later, they're clearing out the last rounds and holstering their weapons before making the trek back through the forest and climbing into Jay's truck.

"Should we give Mike a head's up?" Jay asks turning over the ignition.

"Nah, he was being called in at the same time."

The building is a shit show when Mike, Jay, and Parker finally walk through the revolving glass doors.

"Davis! Miller! Collins!" Inspector Porter yells from the bank of elevators, "My office!"

"Shit, what'd you do, man?" Jay and he look accusingly at Mike. The three of them almost never get called into Porter's office and if they do it usually has something to do with a stupid stunt Mike pulled. Sometimes the guy still thinks he's five.

Mike lifts his arms and shrugs. "I didn't do anything this time."

"This time," Jay huffs.

If they thought downstairs was a shit show, then what they see when they step off the elevator on the top floor must be a cluster fuck or would it be a goat fuck? He never knows which one is which and he has no time to debate the difference with the guys now because the inspector looks down right pissed when the three of them enter his office. His posture is rigid while he sits behind his mahogany desk and he's constantly running a hand through his neatly cropped, dark hair.

"Have a seat, boys." Porter doesn't look up from the open file on his desk until all three of them have taken a seat in the chairs across from him, and even then, he lets them squirm for a few more seconds before clearing his throat, and bores his brown eyes into each of theirs. "All three of you and your teams are up for assignment. You all will be going in on this one."

He almost laughs out loud when Mike lets out an audible sigh of relief next to him, knowing he wasn't the cause of them getting called into Porter's office.

Porter slaps down three identical folders and signals for them to each to grab one. "This is your priority. I'll reassign any open cases you three still have. I want all hands on deck for this one."

"Jennifer White," Jay reads.

"Murdered?" Parker looks at Porter for confirmation.

"Her body was just found in a Provincial Park nearby. Her parents are highly respected lawyers in Ontario. In fact, her dad's running for Prime Minister this election."

"What does our team have to do with the case? We don't work murders," Mike states.

"The MO is the same as several cases dating back to 2000 and ranging from Ontario, to Alberta, to here in BC. Except they keep getting more sophisticated. More organized."

"You think we're looking at a serial killer," Jay clarifies.

"Was there a murder weapon?" Parker asks, glancing back through the information in the report.

"Cause of death is strangulation."

"Why isn't homicide looking into this?" Mike asks what they're all wondering.

"It's officially become a cross-jurisdictional case. She was dumped here, but they believe she was killed in Alberta. Her parents are insisting they want the best of the best on this case. The top dogs tend to agree since this could have a potential blowback on the RCMP if we don't solve this in a reasonable time frame. They want every available team on this."

"There's not a lot of evidence here." Jay holds up his file.

"No, there's not. I need you guys to do what you do best. Find this guy and take him out."

Parker, Jay, and Mike exchange a look of understanding before turning to Porter and nodding their acceptance of the case.

"Your team will be reassigned to Homicide for this case. They've already been told that the three of you will be running the show from now on. I'll leave it to the three of you to delegate your teams but I want reports every few hours."

All three of them nod.

"Good, now get to work." Porter dismisses them with a tip of his chin towards the door.

CHAPTER SIX

"How did that make you feel, Danielle?"

Ashley hates when they fucking ask her that stupid question. She stares at the shrink sitting across from her in her big, leather chair.

She crosses her arms and grumbles, "Fine."

"Just fine?"

"Yes."

Dr. Stevenson says nothing while she stares at her, her pen hovering above the annoying, yellow legal pad, waiting for her to elaborate more, but she doesn't. Why should she waste the breath? There's no way she'll spill her thoughts to a shrink anyway.

If she hadn't promised Kat almost a year ago she'd at least give counselling a chance, then she wouldn't have to be in this stupid office, sitting on this stupid, floral couch, talking to this shrink.

Finally, she must realize she's not going to elaborate because Dr. Stevenson sighs and puts the legal pad and pen back on her desk before turning back.

"Danielle, if you were fine then you wouldn't be here, would you?"

"I'm only here because I promised my best friend I'd give you a shot."

"Why did you promise her that?"

Because Kat has been bugging her for close to a year to talk to someone professional. Because the nightmares have come back with a vengeance.

But she doesn't say any of that. She just shrugs, refusing to react to Dr. Stevenson and her questions. Her eyes are glued to the clock above the shrink's head, and as soon as the hour strikes, she's up and has her hand on the door handle ready to get out of here.

"See you next week," Dr. Stevenson calls out before the door swings closed behind Ashley.

Un-fucking-likely.

"Dinner's ready!" Kat calls from the kitchen as Ashley walks through the front door of their condo. It's been a little over eleven months since they moved into their new place across the country.

"I'm not hungry." That's a lie.

She can't force herself to eat right now. She's too agitated. After leaving Dr. Stevenson's office she felt the hairs on the back of her neck stand up. When she turned around she could've sworn she saw Adam following her. She'd picked up her pace and ducked into a nearby coffee shop but when she glanced back he wasn't anywhere to be seen.

Maybe she was hallucinating, or maybe he'd been able to track her down despite all the effort she, Kat, and Alice had gone through to change their names and appearance.

"I brought lasagna home from the restaurant," Alice chimes in from the couch as she flips through *Cosmopolitan* magazine.

"Nah, I'm good. I stopped for a salad after my appointment."

"I put a plate in the fridge for you for later," Kat adds when she joins them on the couch with a plate piled high with lasagna and Caesar salad.

"Thanks."

"So how'd it go at Dr. Stevenson's?"

Ashley shrugs "Okay, I guess." *Except I think I saw Adam when I left.*

"We should go out tonight. It's ladies' night at Gotcha's, and I'm ready to get my drink on," Alice says, closing the magazine and turning to face her and Kat.

Ashley wants to hug her right now for changing the subject away from her appointment.

"You're always ready to get your drink on, Alice." Kat laughs, then glances at Ashley and suddenly she looks uncertain as to whether she should accept Alice's invite or decline and offer to stay home with her.

But Ashley knows what she's doing. Kat still thinks she can't be around alcohol without feeling the temptation to drink until she blacks out. Usually she would be making excuses to stay home, but right now she needs to get out of her own head for several hours.

She could use a little temptation tonight, whether it's a whiskey on the rocks or something tall, dark, and handsome. She would happily welcome either option.

"Let's do it!" She exclaims patting their knees before jumping up to go raid her closet.

"Oh, I messaged Mike, the friend I was telling you about, the guy who helped us find this place. He's with the RCMP and said he's willing to talk to you about your situation," Alice calls from the living room.

Ashley is utterly confused. She wasn't aware Alice's friend was part of the RCMP.

She pokes her head out of her bedroom, "You didn't need to do that, Alice. I mean, we moved across the country, changed our names, and our appearance." She counts off on her fingers then shrugs. "What more is there to do?"

"Mike could offer some advice on things we've never thought of and . . ." Alice quickly sends a message from her phone before lifting her head to Ashley, "he already said he'll meet us at the club with a couple of guys from his team."

She groans and rolls her eyes. "You're impossible."

"But you love me," Alice sing songs, walking to her bedroom.

"Unfortunately," She mutters under her breath.

"I heard that!" Alice yells from her room.

"You were supposed to!" She yells back grinning.

CHAPTER SEVEN

Gotcha's is packed wall to wall with bodies. Ladies night at the club is always a gong show but it's even more crazy tonight.

"Hell yes!" Mike exclaims next to Parker as his eyes roam over all of the scantily clad women dancing around them. "Dude, I think I've died and gone to heaven."

"Amen, brother," Jay agrees while they push their way across the dance floor and over to the bar.

As they're waiting for the four-people deep line at the bar to die down so they can order their drinks, Parker's gaze lands on, and travels up, a pair of gorgeous, long legs up to a finely shaped ass encased in a short, black dress that has molded itself perfectly to luscious curves. Long, black hair flows over one shoulder, and soulful, green eyes stare back at him. Holy shit. He feels like he just got punched in the gut; all the air in his lungs suddenly leaves him.

It doesn't last long though because Mike is slapping Parker on the shoulder.

"Dude, let's just go to the booth and get one of the girls to bring over our drinks. This line is nuts."

Before Parker turns to follow Mike and Jay to their usual booth he glances back over his shoulder to get another look at the beauty, but she's no longer there.

It will be a miracle if Ashley manages not to break an ankle in these stiletto heels by the end of the night, especially with how packed the club is.

"Finally! What took you so long?" Alice yells over the loud thump of the base as she slips back into the booth, placing three tequila shots in the middle of the table.

"Line at the bar was crazy." She rolls her eyes. "Next time you can get your own drink," she yells back.

Alice and Kat go back to finishing their conversation while she tries to subtly scan the crowd in an effort to locate the guy from the bar.

He was sexy with those bluer than the Pacific eyes, five o'clock shadow, and square jaw. She feels giddy with the possibility she may have found the distraction she's looking for tonight.

"Ash! Ash! Ashley!" Kat yells above the music trying to get her attention.

"What?"

"We asked you if you wanted to come dance with us. But it looks like you're a little distracted." Alice grins. Apparently she wasn't as subtle as she thought.

"I was trying to find this really hot guy I saw at the bar, but this crowd is nuts." She leans back against the back of the booth giving up her search. There's no way she's going to find him again tonight.

Alice shrugs. "Bummer, but I'm going to get another shot and then get my ass on the dance floor. You ladies coming?"

"I thought you were texting Mike to see where he's at," Kat says.

"I did. He said they're here. I told him where to find us but I'm not going looking for them in this crowd," Alice replies before sliding out of the booth and pushing her way through to the bar while Ashley and Kat follow behind.

They're waiting for the now five-people deep line at the bar to die down so they can order their drinks when Alice's phone lights up. Her head snaps up and looks from side to side before waving at someone in one of the private booths.

"Over there," Alice turns back to her and Kat and points over her shoulder towards the upstairs booth before turning on her heels and making her way through the crowd.

Ashley starts to feel extremely claustrophobic with all the bodies crammed into the club and very little breathing room.

Shouldn't there be a person limit to this place?

"Ladies."

She hears an extremely sexy voice call out when she peeks around Alice's shoulder.

"Mike, Nicole and Danielle. Ladies, Mike and—"

"Jay." Mike's equally sexy friend extends his hand for Kat and Ashley to shake. His dark brown hair is cropped short on the side but a bit longer on the top, just enough to grab onto and tug. When his eyes find Ashley's they're an intense emerald color. His black, short-sleeve shirt pulls across the expanse of his chest, showing off an impressive set of pecs There's a tattoo peeking out from under his T-shirt sleeve but it's too dark to make out the design.

Despite their good looks, Jay and Mike still don't compare to the guy she saw at the bar.

"Jay, this is Jessica." Mike tips his head in their direction.

"Thought there was going to be three of you," Alice says, sitting down in the booth next to Mike, while Kat slides in next to Jay.

"Parker's here somewhere." Mike runs a hand through his short, black hair before letting it settle on the booth behind Alice.

"I'm going to dance. You coming?" Ashley looks to Alice then to Kat, but both women shake their heads. She turns and saunters over to the dance floor.

She's in her element on the dance floor as her body moves to the sensual beat of the music. The DJ is on fire tonight.

Strong hands land on her hips and draw her closer to the very masculine body standing in front of her.

When she opens her eyes she's staring into the sexy blue ones of the man from the bar. The corner of his mouth pulls up in a playful grin as one of his eyebrows rises in challenge.

Will she tell him to get lost or will she pull him closer? But this was the exact distraction she was looking for tonight.

She hooks her arm over his shoulder and moves her body closer to his, never missing a beat of the music.

The two of them dance for the next few songs, their bodies in almost constant contact.

He groans. "You'll be the death of me, woman."

She smiles leaning in closer to him. "You haven't seen anything yet."

She takes his hand and leads him off the dance floor in the direction of the women's bathroom. One they're inside, Ashley shuts and locks the door.

She never did get the man's name but that night was definitely one for the memory banks.

Neither did Parker get the name of the woman who blew his mind in the women's bathroom of the night club.

His last prey was unplanned but that was okay. It's been fucking forever since he was able to feel the rush of watching the life leave someone's eyes.

His first victim's weren't green though. They were a horrible, bright blue.

Green eyes. Those were his weakness. A memory of a certain blonde haired, green eyed woman invades his head. Her eyes widened in fear . . . of him.

That was the look that flamed his need to hunt. To kill. And when his mark fights back, a grin spreads across his face, he's never been so turned on his life.

His first victim never did turn him on, but he needed her to help get him the partner position at the law firm. One year. One fucking year he'd been married to the bitch.

It was finally over though; he'd officially been named partner at the firm last month. He's had no real use for her, and then her fucking parents had invited them to their vacation house in British Columbia, forcing him to have to play the devoted son-in-law.

That's when he saw her again. She wasn't a blonde anymore, instead her hair was as dark as night, but he'd recognize those eyes anywhere. He'd finally found her.

This time he wasn't going to let her get away. Ever.

CHAPTER EIGHT

He sits in a darkened corner of the pub watching her. She's oblivious to his eyes following her every move. The bitch thought she could just leave him in the middle of the night. She thought moving across the country would save her from him.

But he'd found her. He'll always find her. Now that that nosy wife of his is out of the picture for good, he can finally claim what was always his.

His blood boils with rage when one of the other male patrons sits down next to his possession. Ashley is his, and that guy will pay for touching what is his, but for now he'll bid his time with someone else to help take the edge off.

Movement out of the corner of his eyes catches his attention. When he turns to investigate, a brunette with eyes so hazel they have flecks of gold in them, smiles at him.

She looks eerily similar to Ashley but for her eyes. His mouth curves up on one side as he tips his glass in greeting.

Looks like he just found his next adrenaline rush. She looks like she'll be a fun conquest. He likes when they put up a fight. It makes it that much more thrilling.

She's sitting in a bar in town an hour outside of her own, contemplating drinking the whiskey sitting in front of her. She didn't have the strength today to not order it.

Today was fucking hard. She thought she'd seen Adam standing outside the bookstore she regularly visits

First the shrink's office, now the bookstore. Maybe she was losing it.

She felt like a weight was pushing down on her insides. She couldn't breathe, and her legs failed to move when he'd stopped inches away from her.

But it wasn't him.

Shivers rake down her spine when a couple from the back of the pub pass behind her.

Her throat burns, and she's struggling to breathe. She can't let that asshole get to her like this. She's worked hard to get to where she is and she's not about to let some doppelganger set her back.

She can't. She won't let it.

"Is this seat taken?"

She looks up into a set of the most gorgeous blue eyes she's ever seen. Recognition dawns when she realizes those same eyes stared back at her across the bathroom stall at Gotcha's night club.

"N-No," she stammers.

When he sits down she takes that opportunity to look at him in the light of day, without the strobe lights.

He's wearing jeans similar to what he wore that night. Her mouth waters at the memory of him bent at the bar and the perfect way those jeans hugged his ass. Then the feel of him inside of her later that night. The guy looks like he's built of solid muscle.

Her eyes take their time roaming up the solid expanse of his chest, noticing the way his black T-shirt pulls tightly across his shoulders and exposes his arms.

Those arms look like they're made to give the most amazing hugs. You know, those hugs that make you instantly feel safe. Like nothing in the world could touch you as long as you stay curled up in them.

When she is finally able to draw her gaze away from lusting over the man's arms, his lips are tugged up on one side, and amusement dances behind his eyes.

"Parker," he sticks his hand out for her to shake.

"Danielle or Dani. My friends call me Dani." She didn't mean for all of that to spill out but she couldn't help it. The man makes her nervous, and when she's nervous she either completely stops talking or she spews verbal diarrhea.

There's no happy medium for her. She wishes there were. If he notices he doesn't let on. He just smiles at her, then his eyes move down to the glass of whiskey she's playing with.

"Do you plan on drinking that or just playing with the glass?" He quips.

She sighs. "I haven't decided yet."

"What's there to decide?" He raises an eyebrow.

"I had a shit day. If I drink it, I may not stop at just one."

"So why order it?"

She looks over at him and into his blue eyes. For some reason she feels like she could tell him the truth. Which is weird, right? Not only did she just meet him a couple of days ago but she fucked him in the bathroom stall at a club, didn't ask his name, and now here he was, looking all sexy and shit.

"Out of habit, I guess."

"Ah well tell you what. If you have just that one drink. I'll make it my personal mission to make sure you don't have any more while we sit here."

"That easy, huh?" She grins.

"Yep. And I'll even tell you a lame pickup line I heard today." He lifts his shoulders in a shrug. "It might make you laugh."

"Pretty sure of yourself," she says, amused.

"There's one condition though." He leans his elbows on the bar looking over at her.

"And what's that?"

"If it does make you laugh, then you go out to dinner with me Friday night."

"And if it doesn't?"

"Then you go out to dinner with me Friday night."

She giggles. "Oh, I don't know. Those are some pretty tough conditions. You sure you can handle it?"

He beams. "Those are the conditions."

"All right, let's hear it."

He leans in closer to her, whispering in her ear. She tries to ignore how good he smells, but it's useless. It's intoxicating, like spent gunpowder and worn leather; it's pure man. It should be illegal, just how good he smells.

"Were you forged by Sauron? 'Cause, baby, you're precious."

She throws her head back and laughs. It's the only way she can think of to move away from him and not make it look awkward. But, seriously, she could bury her nose in the crook of his neck and just inhale his masculine scent all day along.

"Did you just use a *Lord of the Rings* pickup line?"

"Sure did." He grins.

"That's impressive."

He laughs. "You should've seen my face when the old lady at the coffee shop said it to me this morning. I think my jaw hit the floor."

She laughs, and it's a good belly laugh. One she hasn't experienced in a very long time. It feels good.

"I think I earned my date, right?"

She shakes her head, but there's a smile on her face, "You did. Give me your phone."

She extends her hand toward him with her palm up. He obliges, placing his iPhone in her waiting grasp. When she's done entering her information she gives it back to him, stands up, and gathers her coat from the back of the bar stool, along with her purse.

Before making a hasty exit, she briefly turns back to him. "It was nice meeting you, Parker. You made the rest of my day seem not so bad after all."

Before he can manage to get a reply out, she's already walking out the door. Her drink is still sitting on the bar, untouched and forgotten.

She grins when her phone pings with a new message.

Parker: Glad I could help. I'll pick you up at 6 p.m.

Tonight couldn't have come any faster. It's only been three days since Parker saw Danielle at the pub, and she'd agreed to dinner with him. Three days that seemed to drag on.

He hated lying to the guys about having to work late tonight but he didn't want to tell them about her yet. He wanted her to himself for a bit.

She was different from all the other women he'd introduced to them. None of his relationships, if you could call them that, lasted more than a weekend. He liked the freedom of not being tied down. But one look into those eyes and he already knew he was going to be out his element with this woman.

She opens her condo door, and a corner of her mouth quirks up in a smile when she sees him.

"Hi! How'd you get in the building?"

"Somebody was leaving as I was walking up. I saw your name and condo number on the buzzer." He shrugs his shoulders, returning her smile.

"Well, do you want to come in? Nic and Jess aren't home. I just have to grab my purse and keys." She steps back and opens the door wider but doesn't wait around for his decision before she turns away and walks towards what he assumes must be her bedroom.

Her place doesn't look at all like what he would've pictured a woman's place to look like. Except for the throw blanket strewn across the back of the couch and the two colorful pillows, the furniture is all clean, sleek lines, and all the same black color—the kind of furniture you'd find in a modern furniture store.

His gaze lands on the 70-inch TV attached to the wall and trails down to the entertainment centre where he can make out a PS4, an X-Box One, and multiple pairs of 3D glasses.

He may have just found the woman of his dreams.

When she walks back out of her bedroom in those tight as fuck skinny jeans and black heels, it's all he can do to not say fuck it and suggest they stay here and order in.

On the one hand he's excited to show her off, but on the other he'll have to kill any man who so much as looks at her.

When she bends down to pick her purse up off the floor, he struggles to hold back a groan.

"So where are we going?" She straightens back up and turns to face him. Her hair piled up in a messy bun with tendrils framing her face makes her light eyes pop even more against her dark hair and olive skin.

"If I tell you then where's the fun in that?"

"Fair enough,"

"You ready?"

She grabs her leather jacket from the hallway closet then leads the way to the front door.

CHAPTER NINE

Parker pulls his black Lexus RX 350 up to the curb of a well-known seafood restaurant. Blue's is usually always booked up and takes reservations six to twelve months in advance. Ashley's a little impressed and a bit intrigued as to how he was able to get them a table tonight.

Jogging around to the passenger side of his car and opening the door for her, he offers his hand to help her out.

"Thank you."

"How do you feel about seafood?" he asks, resting his hand on the small of her back and leading her into the restaurant.

"Love it. I grew up eating fresh seafood straight off the boat."

"Hey, Parker," the hostess greets as they approach her stand.

"Anne." He hugs her. "How's Bella doing?"

"Much better now, thank you."

"Glad to hear it."

"Your table is just this way." Anne grabs two menus and leads them over to their table in a secluded area of the restaurant.

"Your waiter will be right over, but can I get some drinks started for you?"

She orders a pinot grigio, and he orders a whiskey on the rocks. Anne writes down their orders before walking over to the bar and back to the hostess stand.

"Come here often?" Ashley teases, glancing up from her menu.

Parker slowly puts his menu down on the table, looking over at her. "Not really. Anne and I grew up together, but we lost touch in tenth grade after her family moved away. We ran into each other again at the hospital last year. Her little sister, Bella, was having her appendix removed, and my grandfather had broken his hip."

He shrugs. "I stayed with Anne in the waiting room while Bella was in surgery. We kept in touch after that."

"Was there anything between you two?"

She mentally chastises herself for asking the question. It wasn't any of her business if Anne and Parker used to be involved.

"Me and Anne? No. I only ever saw her as a little sister. A few weeks after we reconnected at the hospital, her husband, Carl, left her. Anne was working here at the time, trying to make ends meet while raising her sister. I offered to stay with Bella on the nights she had to work. As a thank you, she told me there'd always be a table reserved for me whenever I wanted to eat here. I haven't taken her up on the offer until now."

"It's just the two of them?"

"Their parents died in a car crash two years ago. Anne was twenty-two so she was able to take over guardianship of Bella."

The waiter comes by with the drinks and takes their order. He orders calamari for them as a starter and a lobster for himself, while she orders the seafood fettucine.

"Wow, that's a lot for a twenty-two-year-old to take on."

He nods. "It was, but she didn't want Bella to end up in the system. Bella was three at the time of the crash. Most families who adopt are looking for newborns. Bella would've jumped from foster home to foster home. Anne took over guardianship, picked up a second job, working at the local library before she comes here for the dinner rush.

"She's also enrolled in online classes and is doing her nursing practicum at the hospital during the week. When I heard her story I didn't mind staying with Bella those nights Anne had to work. She's a good kid. Sometimes if Anne has to work at the library and then pulls a double shift here Bella will just stay the night at my place."

He brushes it off like it's no big deal, but it is. Not many people she knows would've stepped up and helped someone like he has with Anne and Bella.

Her heart breaks for the little five-year-old who lost both parents in the blink of an eye, but she's amazed by the strength Anne has shown in taking care of her sister while working two jobs, attending classes, and going through a divorce.

Dinner goes by in a blur. She doesn't remember eating any of her meal, but it must have been amazing because when the waiter comes back to collect their dishes, there isn't a speck of food left on either plate.

The conversation between them is easy. There are no awkward pauses, and it turns out they have a lot in common. He confesses to seeing her gaming systems back at the condo and expresses an interest in going one-on-one in *Call of Duty*. She teases him that she'd be able to kick his butt so they agreed that one-night he would bring over pizza and they'd play.

He leans back in his chair as his eyes roam the restaurant. "Shit," he says, laughing.

"What?"

His blue eyes find her emerald ones, and there's a hint of amusement playing in them. "We're the last ones here."

She lets her eyes gaze around the restaurant as well, and he's right. They're the only customers in the restaurant. Anne is over at the bar talking to the bartender, but there's no one else in sight. "So we are," she says giggling.

"I like that sound."

"What sound?"

"Your laugh."

"Oh." She feels a blush creep into her cheeks.

He pulls his wallet from his suit jacket and throws some bills on the table. She's not great at math but even she can tell there's way more there than what their meal would have cost.

"Come on, let's get out of here." He stands offering her his hand.

As they're about to push through the front door of the restaurant Anne stops them.

"Parker?"

"What's up?"

"Um, I got asked to work a double on Wednesday during the day. Usually Bella would be in school, and then Mrs. Smith from next door would pick her up and keep her until I'm done, but she's going out of town the day before to see her sister and . . ." Anne starts fiddling with the cuffs of her shirt like they're the most fascinating thing in the world.

"I can pick up Bella. It's no problem, Anne. I told you if you ever needed help I'd be happy to entertain her for a few hours. Plus, I owe that munchkin a few rounds of *Little Big Planet.*"

Anne's head snaps up and she grins. "She doesn't like that game this week. She's all about *Paw Patrol* TV show now."

He groans, and Ashley tries very hard to keep in the laugh that's threatening to spill out at any moment.

That is something she's got to see. Actually, she'd pay to see that. This big macho man sitting on his couch watching animated puppies in uniform rescuing baby sea turtles.

His eyes snap to hers. "What's so funny?"

"Picturing you sitting on your couch watching *Paw Patrol.*"

Anne is giggling next to her, too.

"Yeah, yeah. Laugh it up, but when you meet Bella you won't

be laughing anymore."

"Wait, what?" The smile instantly slips from Ashley's face.

"You heard me. You're watching *Paw Patrol* with us." He jokes.

"Ah, no, I'm not. I just met Anne. She probably doesn't want a strange woman hanging around her kid sister."

Anne shrugs. "If Parker trusts you, then I'm fine with it. Bella would probably love having another younger woman around since she has to spend almost all her time with Mrs. Smith when I'm not there. She's great and all but she's getting pretty old now."

His mouth lifts on one corner, and now he's doing everything he can to not laugh at her failed attempt to get out of babysitting.

Before she can think of another way out of it, he places his hand against the small of her back and leads her out of the restaurant and to his car. The gentle touch of his hand on her lower back is enough to cloud her mind and suddenly she's not sure what she was about to protest against.

Damn, this man

How is it possible he can distract her so easily with just one touch?

She tries to steal a glance over at him in the darkness of the car. His one hand is thrown lazily over the steering wheel while the other rests on the gear shift in between their seats. He even makes driving look sexy.

He has long, calloused fingers and manly hands. The kind of hands she's dreamt about caressing her body. Doing dirty things to her. Her pussy clenches and there's a damp spot on her panties from the memory of his hands devouring her at the club.

She does the only thing she can think of to try and distract herself from thinking those thoughts about the man sitting next to her. She starts humming and grins when he takes his eyes off the road for a split second, looking over at her in horror.

"Are you—"

"Paw patrol. Paw patrol. We'll be there on the double . . ."

He groans when she starts singing the opening lines of the show and then chuckles. "I'm not sure I even want to know how you know the opening song."

She shrugs. "I used to babysit with my best friend last summer, before I got my current job."

"And what's that?" He pulls into an empty parking at the beach and cuts the engine before turning in his seat to face her.

"Right now I work in restorative justice but I'll be graduating with my master's in psychology this semester."

He's trying extremely hard to pay attention to the words coming out of her mouth but all he can focus on are her lips and wanting to kiss her again.

The air crackles with unbridled attraction. Her breath hitches when he gently strokes his thumb over her lips, but the sound of waves crashing on the beach breaks the tension in the car.

He pulls away and exhales. "Come on." Stepping out of the car the salty ocean air immediately assaults his senses and he inhales it deeply.

Home.

The only time he's ever felt at home was when he was out on the ocean, on his board riding wave after wave for hours on end.

Back in high school Parker, Jay, and Mike would get up at the ass crack of dawn and come down to catch some waves before heading to their classes for the day. He doesn't remember when it all changed, but it's been years since any of them were on a board.

"It's so peaceful out here," she says when he comes up behind her, wrapping his arms around her belly.

"I love it here. I used to sneak out and come surfing when I needed to clear my head."

He takes a hold of her hand, intertwining their fingers and leads her further down the beach to a more secluded area. He opens the backpack he grabbed from the car and lays down a blanket then motions for her to sit.

When she's comfortable he hands her one of the beers he brought and sits down behind her, placing his legs on either side of hers. She shivers and leans back into him.

"Cold?"

"My feet are a little." She laughs, moving further back into him. "I threw my heels in the car when I saw where we were. Heels and sand don't make a good combination."

He pulls out another blanket from the backpack and lays it over her feet and legs.

"How's that?"

"Better. Thank you." She sighs, leaning her head back against his shoulder.

"Have you lived in Oceanview your whole life?"

"No, I'm from Ontario. About one year ago Nic, Jess, and I

decided we needed a change of scenery. I needed to start over in a city where nobody knew me and they followed."

"Why'd you need to start over?"

"Long story. Maybe sometime I'll tell you." A sad smile tugs at her mouth.

He rests his chin on her shoulder and stares out at the waves crashing onto shore. "I'd like that."

"What about you?"

"Born and raised."

She snuggles further into him, causing his arms to wrap more securely around her. Her strawberry-vanilla scent engulf his senses.

She swiftly turns around and straddles his lap, crushing her mouth to his. Her lips are just as soft as he remembers. Before she can pull away he slips his hand into her hair and holds her to him, continuing the kiss. His tongue traces the seam of her bottom lip, coaxing her to open for him, and she does.

She tastes so damn good, like sweet wine. His dick jumps in his jeans when she wraps her arms around his neck and pushes her breasts into his chest. She moans when he nips at her bottom lip then licks the sting away.

She tries to climb even higher in his lap, causing him to feel her warmth through both of their jeans. Fuck.

His body is a war of want and need. His brain screams at him to slow it down and put an end to it before things progress any further, but his dick is screaming at him to fuck her.

His body wants to relive the way hers moved with his. The way her back arched when he entered her for the first time. But his brain and his heart want to get to know the girl behind the sexy body.

God, does he ever want to take her right here and now, but if he does then she'll just end up being like the other women he's dated.

Her hand leaves his neck and travels down his stomach to the button on his jeans. He grabs her hand, halting her progress, and ends the kiss.

Ashley pulls back, her eyes searching his, but when he doesn't make a move to continue the kiss she hangs her head in defeat and moves to climb off his lap,

"I'm sorry. I shouldn't have—"

He grabs her hands and pulls her back down to him. "Just so

we're clear, because I can see the doubt in your eyes right now, I am interested. Fuck, I'm very interested."

"Okay," she replies but she doesn't sound very convinced.

"We'll get there, babe. But when I have you again it won't be a quick fuck on the beach. No matter how romantic sex on the beach sounds, it's not. I'm not about to get sand in places it should never be getting into. We clear?"

"We're clear."

He tips her chin up with his index finger. "I'm never going to make you do anything you don't want to, Danielle."

"Okay."

"Let's get you home. The tide's starting to come in, and it's freezing out here."

When they leave the beach they're unaware of the shadow that lurks behind the rocks, watching them. Lips pull back in a snarl and fists clench.

CHAPTER TEN

Parker drops her back off at her condo a little after eleven, but she doesn't feel like calling it a night yet. She's actually enjoying being with him, and it doesn't feel like a first date. In fact, it feels like they've known each other for years. She feels comfortable around him and she thinks it's the same for him.

"Want to come in for a drink?"

He shoves his hands in his pockets. "I'd love to but if I go in there I won't be leaving until the morning."

"Oh." She sigh disappointedly, turning to unlock the condo door. "Well, I had fun."

When she turns back around, he has a grin on his face and there's amusement dancing in his eyes. She could stare into those blue eyes all day.

When his hand comes up to stroke her cheek she doesn't hesitate to lean into his touch, taking in as much of his heat as she can. She loves the feel of his hands on her skin. His fingers wrap around the hair at the back of her neck, and he leans down brushing his lips against hers in a light kiss.

"I mean what I said, Dani. I'm very interested," he whispers in her ear, his breath warm against her skin. "Sweet dreams." He presses another soft kiss to her lips before straightening up and walking back down the hallway towards the elevators.

Her head is still foggy from that sweet goodnight kiss, and when she enters the condo and locks the door behind her she doesn't notice the single, long-stemmed, red rose sitting on the dining room table.

"So how'd it go?" Kat asks, placing the wine bottle on the table before dropping down on the couch next to Ashley.

"How'd what go?" Alice asks, walking in to the living room with three white wine glasses.

"Ashley had a date last night."

"What? With whom?"

"Don't know. She won't spill any details about the mystery guy." Kat playfully pouts.

"Come on guys, can we just watch *Criminal Minds* and drink

wine?" Ashley laughs.

"As much as I want to stare at sexy Derek Morgan for ten hours, I think we'd much rather hear the juicy details about your date."

Alice plops herself down on the other side of Ashley.

Alice and Kat are both staring at her, and Ashley knows they're not going to let her get away with at least not telling them something.

"Fine," she huffs. "We went to Blue's for dinner, then we went to sit on the beach for a bit and talked." She shrugs. "It was nice. I like him."

"So you're seeing him again?" Alice nudges her arm.

"I think so. I hope so." Leaning forward she fills all three wineglasses then leans back into the couch. "Now, can we please watch Derek Morgan? I'm going through withdrawals."

"Agreed," Kat and Alice say in unison, reaching for their own wineglasses.

Four hours later all three of them are sitting on the edge of their seats watching as Hotch goes flying back from a car bomb.

"Oh, shit." Alice says.

"Fuck! That's the end of the season?" Kat exclaims.

"I'll get more wine, you guys cue up season four." Ashley jumps up from the couch and races to the kitchen.

She doesn't hear her phone ping with a new message that night. But when she checks her messages the next morning, her heart races and nausea rolls through the stomach. There's no way he could've found her, is there?

Unknown: It doesn't matter how far you run from me; you can change your name, your appearance, you can choose to hide. But I will find you, Ashley. And he won't be able to save you.

CHAPTER ELEVEN

"Dude, what happened to you last night?" Mike hands Parker a beer when he enters Mike's kitchen.

"Stayed late at the station."

"Again?" Jay asks, cracking open his own beer.

Parker shrugs. "Who's playing today?"

"Canucks and Predators," Mike calls over his shoulder as he leads them into the living room.

Mike's living room is the ultimate man cave. Hockey and football memorabilia decorate the walls, an X-box sits on the entertainment stand with various RPG and first shooter games as well as various controllers and gaming headphones strewn about. An 80-inch TV is attached to the wall above the stand playing the usual pre-game line up.

"So who do you thinks going to take this one?" Jay asks, dropping into one of the recliners on either side of the couch.

Mike and Parker glare at him like he's lost his mind. There's only one answer to that question and it's not Nashville.

"What? Nashville could take this one. They're not doing too badly this season."

"I'm going to choose to ignore that." Mike points his beer bottle at Jay and scowls.

Nashville doesn't pull off the win and Vancouver walks away with a 7-3 lead.

This week has gone by in a blur with her doing copious amounts of research for her thesis. She can't wait for graduation to get here so she can finally relax and spend a few days lying around the condo in her pajamas with a *Big Bang Theory* marathon.

She'd just made it back from grabbing a coffee at the Starbucks down the street and was about to power up her laptop to do some research for her forensic psychology class when her phone pings with a message.

Parker: Pick you up in 20.

Crap what day is it?

She quickly closes the message app and brings up the calendar. Wednesday, April 10th. *Shit, it's Wednesday.* She totally forgot he was dragging her along with him while he babysits Bella for Anne today.

Danielle: I can't today, I'm sorry. Thesis due Friday.

Parker: I'll buy coffee and help you study after Anne picks up Bella.

Argh, he brought out the big guns right away. She can never say no to coffee. Let alone free coffee.

Danielle: You had me at coffee.

He pulls up to the curb just as she's pushing her way through the door of the condo building.

"Hey, beautiful." He steps out of the car and walks around to the passenger side opening the door for her.

"Hey, yourself."

"What? No hey, handsome?" he teases as he eases the Lexus back into traffic.

"You haven't earned that level yet." She shakes her head, grinning.

"Oh, I see how it is. We'll just have to change that now, won't we?"

"I guess we will."

He slides his hand closer to hers and intertwines their fingers as they fall into a comfortable silence while "Canadian Girls" by Dean Brody plays through the car's stereo system.

The school they pull up to is huge and nothing like she expected a kindergarten to look like.

"They have kindergarten through grade eight here," he supplies from the driver's seat.

"It's huge."

"Bella loves it. She gets to play with the big kids. Anne's afraid if she keeps hanging around the older kids they might trample her, she's so tiny, but Bella refuses to listen." He laughs. "She says the kids in her class are boring."

"I never knew kindergarteners could be boring." She laughs.

"Bella is very mature for her age. I brought her a doll when she was in the hospital. She rolled her eyes at me and told me she wasn't two anymore. Then she pulled out a book Anne had brought her and proceeded to read me a story. I don't think I've ever had a five-year-old roll their eyes at me."

"Sounds like she's got a bit of attitude too." She giggles.

The bell rings and the doors are pushed open with hundreds of kids pouring out of them. A little girl, five years old, steps off to the side and scans the crowd. She's wearing jeans and a blue Elsa shirt. Her dirty-blonde hair is laying in ringlets around her face, and her blue eyes go wide when they land on Parker, a huge smile spreads across her face when she shoots forward and runs right into his waiting arms.

"Parker!"

"Hey, monkey!" He wraps his arms around Bella and stands up.

"I'm not a monkey!" Bella giggles and squishes his face in her small hands.

He glances down and tickles her. "Hey, what's this?" he asks pointing to her shirt. "I thought you liked *Paw Patrol* not *Frozen*."

Bella rolls her eyes at him. "*Paw Patrol* was so last week, Parker."

"Oh, I'm sorry, princess."

Bella giggles and throws her arms around his neck. "I like being a princess."

Bella only notices Ashley standing there after she unwraps her arms. The look she gives Ashley makes her want to laugh. It's protective and very territorial. Apparently, she doesn't like sharing him with anyone, and she doesn't blame her. She wouldn't want to share him either.

"Bell, this is my friend Dani," he says, nodding towards her.

"Hi, Bella. It's nice to meet you." Ashley holds out her hand for Bella to shake.

That gets a big toothy grin from her. "You're pretty."

"Thank you." She laughs.

"So, Bell, do you think you'd want to hang with Dani and me for the afternoon?" he asks, tickling her sides, causing her to laugh again.

"Is my sister working?"

"Yeah, monkey, she is. But she'll be home in time to tuck you in."

"Can we have pizza?"

He sighs. "Only if you tell your sister we had a big salad with it."

Once they get Bella secured in her booster seat and are on the road again Ashley looks questioningly at him.

"Anne is a little bit of a health nut. She doesn't mind Bella having junk food on occasion as long as it's accompanied by a bowl of fruit or vegetables."

"Parker, can we go swimming?" Bella yells from the backseat.

"We'll see, Bell. I don't think Dani brought her swimsuit."

"Maybe she can go get it or she can borrow yours." Bella giggles.

Parker and Ashley laugh and try unsuccessfully to distract Bella from the subject of the swimsuit. When she keeps bringing it up and shooting him puppy dog eyes in his rear view mirror, he gives in and they stop by Ashley's place.

When she hurries up the small flight of stairs to the front door she doesn't notice the man in the black sedan parked behind Parker watching her intently.

It takes her less than five minutes to go upstairs and locate her suit before she's back in Parker's car, and they're off to his place. Unaware the sedan has followed them.

CHAPTER TWELVE

Ashley walks out of the bathroom in a sexy as hell, red bikini, and it takes all the strength he has not to openly gawk at her and to will his dick to go down.

Her skin looks so smooth, and her long, black hair cascades in waves over each of her shoulders, concealing her breasts from his view. A script tattoo on her rib cage draws his eye, but he can't make out what it says. His eyes are also drawn her belly button piercing.

"What does your tattoo say?"

She glances briefly down to her ribs before meeting his eyes. "'Scars remind us where we've been, they don't have to dictate where we're going' It's a quote from a character on *Criminal Minds*."

"You have scars, Danielle?" he asks.

"Don't we all?"

"Touché."

"Where's Bella?"

He points to the ceiling above his head. "Probably trying to decide which swimsuit to wear."

She laughs. "It's tough being a girl sometimes. Hey, do you have a shirt I could put over this." She gestures to the string bikini. "I hate swimsuit shopping, and this is from two years ago. Not sure it's appropriate to wear around a five-year-old."

"Uh, yeah, sure."

He's not sure whether to be glad she's decided to cover up or extremely disappointed.

After grabbing a T-shirt from his dresser he runs back downstairs with a grin tugging at his lips. He might be a gentleman, but the light grey T-shirt will still cling to all of Danielle's luscious curves when it gets wet.

As soon as Bella sees him walking into the kitchen she starts jumping up and down chanting, "Pool! Pool! Pool!"

Bella may not be his, and he may just be looking after her as a favor to her sister, but she has him wrapped around her little finger. He swears, if this little girl told him to jump he'd ask her how high.

She's five for Pete's sake! But when he saw her lying in that hospital bed after her surgery and heard about their parents he knew he'd do anything to see her smile, to try and help give her the childhood he never had.

"Monkey, why don't you head downstairs and grab a towel but don't open the pool door. Dani and I will order pizza and be down in a few seconds."

"Okay," Bella says and runs to the basement door.

"I mean it, Bell! Do not open the pool door."

Bella stops midrun, turns to him, and puts her hands on her hips, "I know! I know! Geez." She rolls her eyes at him before turning back around and continuing her run through his house.

"You have a pool in your basement?" Ashley asks after pulling the T-shirt over her bikini-clad body.

"It was the only thing I wanted if I ever bought my own house. A year after I was hired at my job I found this place. Pool included."

"The only thing you wanted in a house was an indoor pool?"

"Yup, who doesn't want to be able to swim year around? Especially during our Canadian winters." He grins.

She laughs. "We barely even get a winter here in Oceanview. You could go swimming in the rain."

He scratches the five o'clock shadow coming in on his chin, pretending to think about it. "I could, but then I might get arrested for public indecency."

"Public indecency?"

"Yeah, you know when I want to swim naked." He grins.

"Oh. Do that often, do you?"

"Parker! I'm ready to go swimming!" Bella yells from downstairs.

Damn, that girl has a pair of lungs on her. She also has really bad timing. When he doesn't answer right away, Bella yells his name again.

"Come on, let's go let her into the pool room before she yells the house down." Slipping his hand into hers he leads them towards the basement door.

Bella is standing at the edge of the pool with her hands on her hips and a pool noodle sticking out from under one arm.

"It's about time you got down here," Bella says accusingly.

"Easy, monkey. I thought I told you to wait at the door?" he asks while grabbing towels for both him and Ashley.

"Sorry." Bella rolls her eyes. "Can I go in now?"

"No, now you can wait until we're both ready. No jumping in unless Danielle or I are in the pool with you," he instructs.

Ashley raises an eyebrow questionably.

"What? She may have me wrapped around her finger, but I won't ever actually tell her that." He laughs.

The three of them play Marco Polo and chase each other around the length of the pool for almost half an hour before Bella decides it would be a good idea if she and Danielle team up and splashed him.

She was right, it was fun at first. Until he started countering all their moves and got ahold of Bella before tossing her and her pool noodle in the shallow part. He did the same thing to Ashley while she squealed and laughed.

They only decided to take a break when the pizza finally arrived and then they stuffed their bellies full.

Ashley's extremely exhausted by the time they flop down on the couch in front of the TV. She glances over at Parker while Bella picks a movie. He looks as exhausted as she feels.

She's not surprised though. He tossed her and Bella into the water a handful of times and then continued to chase Bella around the pool some more. Seeing the two of them together and how much Bella looks up to him pulls at her heart.

"I picked one, Dani," Bella announces as she climbs onto Ashley's lap, remote in hand.

She's warmed up to Ashley a lot over the last several hours, even pouting when she didn't sit next her while they ate. It was so heartbreaking, Ashley actually got out of her seat on the couch and sat next to Bella on the floor with the pizza box in front of them. Parker, the little shit, just laughed.

"Which one did you pick?"

"*Frozen!*" Bella beams up at her.

"Cool! I haven't seen that one yet."

"Elsa's my favourite!"

"Bell, why don't you come sit here and give Dani some more room?" He pats the open space between them, but Bella doesn't budge. Instead, she snuggles in closer to Ashley and wraps her arms around her middle.

"It's okay, she can stay if she wants."

Bella nods and hands him the remote so he can press play.

Elsa is singing about letting something go, and Bella is fast asleep in her lap when the doorbell wakes Ashley She must have fallen asleep at some point during the movie too.

"Hey, Anne. Come on in."

She hears his voice down the hallway, and in the next minute he and Anne are turning the corner into the living room.

"She's asleep." Ashley smiles at Anne.

"Thank you so much, guys. I really appreciate it," Anne says moving to pick up Bella, but Parker stops her.

"I've got her." He scoops up Bella and follows Anne out to her car after she says bye to Ashley. When he comes back inside he flops back onto the couch and opens his arms for her to move closer. She doesn't hesitate to curl up next to him with her head on his chest.

"You owe me a coffee."

"I do."

"Nap time first, though." She yawns.

"Agreed." He already sounds half asleep with his head thrown back against the back of the couch.

"Come on, A. You've been seeing this guy for close to three months now, and we still haven't met him or know who he is," Alice whines

"At least give us a name, Ash." Kat adds.

"Seriously, this is like the fifth girls' night you guys have hounded me about him."

"And we will continue to do so until you give us what we want." Alice grins.

"Yup, 'cause that's what girlfriends are for. Plus, how are we supposed to Facebook stalk the guy and give you our opinions if we don't know his name?" Kat adds.

"Exactly!" Alice agrees.

"Argh. Okay, you are not going to Facebook stalk him." Ashley points to Alice.

"I promise not to stalk him if you spill the beans on who this mystery guy is."

Ashley just shakes her head, not giving into Alice and Kat's inquiries.

Alice huffs and crosses her arms over her chest. "All right, fine. I give up."

"Finally." Ashley grins.

"For now," Alice adds. "Don't forget we're meeting up with Mike and some guys from his team this weekend."

"Still not letting that go, huh?" Ashley asks.

"No. Not until we know for sure Adam won't be able to touch you."

When Ashley leaves the restaurant and walks out to her car to head over to Parker's there's a single, long-stemmed, red rose laying in between her windshield and wiper blades. There isn't a note attached. A small smile pulls at her lips thinking about him sneaking out here and placing the rose on her windshield without telling her.

Parker's in his kitchen, bent over the oven, when Ashley walks in. His ass looks so good in his wranglers.

"Hi, handsome."

"Hi, babe." He turns around with a big grin on his face and oven mitts on both hands, a covered pan held between them.

"What's cookin', good lookin'?"

He shakes his head and raises an eyebrow at her comment.

"What? Not funny?"

"You need some new material."

She shrugs. "I thought it was fine."

The smell of sweet pineapple and sugar waft up from the pan, making her mouth water. "What's for dinner?"

"Ham with a pineapple and brown sugar glaze." He places the pan on the stove and turns back around, pulling off the oven mitts.

"He cooks."

"Come here. I feel like I haven't seen you in months."

She steps into his waiting arms and she feels like she can finally breathe and relax when his arms close around her, his warm breath on her neck.

"That's because it's been too long. I missed this."

"Me too." He places open-mouthed kisses on her neck and

along her jaw line. "You smell incredible."

"You don't smell so bad yourself."

"I just had a shower. You wouldn't have said that ten minutes ago." He chuckles. "The boys and I hit the gym pretty hard tonight."

"Hmm, I don't know. You all sweaty and shirtless?" Her hands run up his gloriously well-built stomach, to his chest, over his shoulders, and down his equally powerful arms. "I think I could get on board with that."

"What else could you get on board with, babe?"

She trails her fingers lightly back down his chest to his stomach and pops open the button of his jeans before cupping him over his underwear. "You fucking me six ways till Sunday."

He groans. "You have some mouth on you."

"Oh, baby, you haven't seen the things my mouth can do."

The more she talks, the more he grows beneath her hand. She's enjoying the power she holds over this man right now. If she wanted to she could probably make him come hard, but she won't. She wants to draw it out a little first. Tease him a bit longer.

"Fuck."

"Me," Ashley supplies for him.

He raises an eyebrow. "You want to do it in the kitchen?"

They've had sex in every room in his house so far, except for the kitchen. He was hoping that maybe today would've been the day she decided to christen this room too.

"Who said anything about fucking in the kitchen?" she asks, dropping her clothes to the floor as she makes her way through the kitchen to the hallway and then up the stairs.

Spinning around when she hears his feet running up the steps two at a time, she reaches behind her and unclasps her black, lace bra before taking it off and tossing at him.

He groans and drops her bra on the top landing before following her into the bedroom

His calloused fingers trail lightly over her smooth, olive skin, moving down her side, her waist, her hip, and her thigh; his mouth placing delicious, open-mouthed kisses along her neck and jaw.

Ashley tilts her chin higher, giving him more access. His warm breath on her skin sends shivers skimming across her body. His touch, his smell, his voice, are a heady combination that leave her breathless.

"You're so sexy," he whispers in her ear.

She crushes her mouth to his, her tongue demanding entry. He groans as his lips part. The kiss is hard. Demanding.

Her fingers skim down his back until they reach the hem of his shirt, and she hurriedly peels it up and over his broad shoulders, their lips part for a split second while his shirt is pulled over his head.

Finally, she's able to feel his skin under her fingers. He's strong and rock hard beneath her touch. She moans as she rakes her fingernails up his back, smirking as he grunts. She doesn't feel guilty at all for leaving her mark on him. He's hers and she doesn't have any intention of sharing him.

He settles even more between her legs when she parts them, wrapping one leg around his waist, pulling him closer.

She can't get enough of this man. She never thought she'd be able to trust another man. She was convinced she would never find love again. But then he came around. What started out as a quick fuck in a club bathroom turned into something magical. And, yes, she's fully aware of how ridiculous and naïve that sounds, but that's what happened.

She never expected to see him again. He was just supposed to be a momentary distraction. Then she saw him at the pub the following week and he asked her to dinner. The rest, as they say, is history. This man showed her what it felt like to laugh again. To love again. He showed her what it felt like to be loved by someone. A feeling she's never experienced with anyone before.

His fingers slip under her black, lace thong, parting her lips. Ashley moans when his finger starts rubbing slow circles on her clit.

Fuck that feels good.

Her hips buck when he increases the pressure and his pace.

"I'm not going to last long if you keep that up," she says, panting.

He chuckles. "Baby, that's my plan. Don't think this will be a one shot night."

He sits back on his knees and lightly drags her thong down her legs, adding to her already heightened senses. His thumb goes back to stroking circles around her clit while he slips a finger inside her.

Her back arches off the bed begging him to go deeper. He adds another finger before giving into her demand. She's so wet, her juices are running down his hand and soaking the bed sheet.

"Fuuck," he groans.

"I'm going to come," she says as she breathes heavily.

"Come for me, babe." He increases his speed, hitting that sweet spot inside of her.

She shuts her eyes and moans his name when she comes. Her breathing hard, her body the most relaxed it's been in a long time.

When she opens her eyes, his are burning with hunger. Maintaining eye contact he brings his fingers to his mouth and sucks them, tasting her on his tongue.

Her fingers fly to the button on his jeans, tugging them down in record speed. He chuckles when she doesn't waste a second pulling down his boxers as soon as his jeans are off.

"Someone's a little eager."

"Fuck yeah," she replies.

She groans when she sees he's already standing at full attention. Fuck he's big.

Her mouth waters as her fingers wrap around him. He's hot and solid in her hand. She can't wait to feel him inside of her. He groans when she flicks her tongue up his length, base to tip, then runs it along the slit.

He hisses as her lips wrap around his length, taking him into her mouth inch by inch. She twirls her tongue around his head when she pulls back before sucking him deeply again.

"Fuck," he growls when she repeats the motion. "I really need to be inside you, Dani."

She smirks, standing up and gathering her hair over one shoulder before turning around and bending over the bed, offering her ass up to him.

The smoldering look she throws him over her shoulder is almost his undoing but he holds it together long enough to tear open the condom wrapper and slide it on.

He inserts one finger then a second inside her, making sure she's still ready to take him. When he's satisfied she's wet enough, he strokes his cock once then twice, before lining up the head with her entrance.

She takes all of him, and when he's fully seated inside her pussy, he gives her a couple of seconds to adjust to his length. She moans when he withdraws then pushes in again. She's so tight, he has to consciously remind himself to slow down or he's going to come too fast.

It's only seconds later he feels her pussy constrict around his cock, and she's coming again, hard. His own release follows not far behind.

They both collapse in a sweaty heap on the bed after he disposes of the condom in the bathroom garbage can.

It's early the next morning before sleep finally comes for them. Parker was true to his word about it not being a one shot night.

If that was what sex was supposed to feel like, then she certainly wasn't going to complain. She could probably get used to marathon sex with him.

CHAPTER THIRTEEN

"Holy shit," Ashley says, taking in the large, brick house looming in front of them.

A stone pathway sits in the middle of a well-manicured lawn, leading up to a wraparound porch, where a double-swing sits to the side of the French front doors. A three car garage sits atop the long driveway

"How many vehicles does one person need?" Kat asks taking in a matte-black Ducati sitting in between a black Ford F-150 with red outlining the rims, and a red and black Toyota Tundra.

Alice laughs. "Only the Ford is Mike's. The other two belong to his teammates. And to answer your question, Mike has a Kawasaki, and an Audi R8 he never drives. But oddly enough, he's always washing the damn thing."

The women laugh as Mike opens the front door.

"Ladies," he greets, opening the door wider for them to pass through. "Would any of you like a beer?"

"Sure," all three of them respond, following him down the hallway and into his kitchen.

Mike's house is nothing like Ashley expected. The entire place looks like it was decorated by a professional designer. Mike's kitchen is huge; white cupboards and grey, granite countertops sit against every wall in the room. The center island spans the entire length of the kitchen.

When they round the corner, Ashley's eyes land on a very familiar set of blue ones.

"Ladies, these are some of my team members. You've met Jay but this is—"

"Parker," Ashley supplies.

"Danielle." Parker grins.

"You two have met?" Alice asks.

Ashley turns to Alice with a sigh. "It's Parker."

"Yeah, we've established that," Kat chimes in.

Ashley widens her eyes at Kat in silent communication, but it's Alice who gets it first.

"No way. The guy you've been seeing is Parker?" Alice laughs.

Jay and Mike have settled against the counter with beers in their hands and grins on their faces, enjoying the show.

Parker is still smiling like an idiot, amused watching Danielle try to explain to her friends how she knows him.

That smile fades when he realizes why they're all here. All Mike had told them was that Jess had a friend who was in trouble with an ex of hers and she needed help or advice on what to do to protect her safety.

He'd mentioned that Jess's friend had already moved across the country and had changed her name and appearance. But Jess was still worried about the ex finding her and following her out here.

If Danielle was the friend, then it meant she'd lied to him about potentially everything. Anger starts crawling its way up his spine. He hoped that maybe it wasn't Danielle who Mike was referring to. Maybe it was the other friend, what was her name? Nicole.

His hope is dashed with Mike's next question.

"So, Danielle, what can we help you with?"

He clenches his jaw, grinding his teeth in the process, and crosses his arms over his chest. She fucking lied to him.

This is why he never put the effort into dating a woman. They always lied to him in some way. Never being completely honest with him. He didn't have time for people like that, not just women. Trust was everything to him.

Ashley looks nervously from Mike to Jay and then to him. His whole attitude towards her has gone cold. The smile that played at his lips when she first entered the kitchen is long gone, now his face is just a mask. Ashley can't tell what he's thinking.

Why did she let Alice talk her into doing this? She already had everything under control. There was no way Adam was going to find her out here.

She glances back over at Parker. He's still wearing his poker face, but pure hatred is radiating off him in waves now.

Nausea rolls through her. "I'm sorry, I can't do this." She bolts out of the kitchen, back down the hallway, and out the front door, collapsing onto the lawn as soon as she inhales the fresh air.

The nausea backs off, but fear takes its place.

She's afraid if Parker knew the real her, he'd walk out the door and never come back. They'd only been seeing each other for a little over three months, but she was falling for him.

She cares more about him than she'd ever cared for anyone before, including Adam. Yet, every time he's tried to ask her about her past she'd distract him and change the subject. She hates talking about her past and having to relive those memories.

Also, she's certain that if he knew the truth about her past there was no way he'd keep wasting his time on her. And she's selfish. She wants whatever's happening between them to last just a little longer. She knows she'll have to tell him sooner or later if they ever had a hope of a future, but when she does, he'll leave. They all eventually leave.

Who's she kidding? From the look on his face, he already knew she'd lied to him.

He feels like a royal ass when Danielle darts out of Mike's kitchen like the house is on fire. He feels like even more of an ass when he looks out the window and sees her collapse on the front lawn.

She's breathing hard, like she's just run a marathon and tears are streaking down her cheeks.

That's the last straw for him. He may be angry she lied to him but he at least owes her time to explain.

"Danielle," he says, kneeling down on the grass next to her. The warm summer sun beating down on them.

When she looks up at him with eyes full of sadness and regret, he wishes he could just forget about finding out she lied to him.

"I'm sorry." She hiccups between sobs.

"Why didn't you just tell me, Danielle?"

"Because I'm fucked up. Because you have the power to break me even worse than I was before, and I don't think I can survive it if you left."

"Baby, you're not fucked up."

She can't stop the tear that escapes from the corner of her eye, but he brushes it away with his thumb before it has a chance to run down her cheek.

"Who hurt you, Danielle?"

She shakes her head, avoiding his eyes. She can't go there right now—with him. The pain and the darkness are still there, barely below the surface, waiting for the chance to explode and consume her again. She can't give in to it now and if she tells him, if she lets him in, she might be letting the darkness in again too.

"Baby, do you trust me?"

She nods her head.

"Then trust me to still be here after you tell me. Trust our relationship to be strong enough to handle it. If we're ever going to have a chance to make this work then I want to know you. It doesn't matter if it's happy or sad or down right depressing. I want to know you. All of you: the past, the present, and the future."

God, she was seriously falling for this man but she meant what she'd said. If he left she didn't think she'd be able to survive being broken again. But he was right, she needed to trust him and their relationship.

"Okay."

"Why don't we get off Mike's front lawn though. We can take my bike back to my place." He stands up, offering her his hand.

When he hands her the extra helmet and straddles the bike, she looks skeptically at the bike and then at him.

He laughs holding out his hand and helping her jump on behind him. "You'll be fine. Just keep your arms wrapped around me."

She takes a deep breath and looks like she's preparing herself to go to battle, and he guesses in some ways she is. He knows this must not be easy for her; over the last three months of getting to know her she's alluded to having a difficult past but would never elaborate further than that.

He's guessed there's been a lot of pain in her past but he wasn't prepared for just how much.

"My entire childhood I always felt like I was a worthless use of space, especially from extended family like grandparents, aunts, and uncles."

She glances up at him, and he nods for her to continue.

"Don't get me wrong, my parents, my cousins, and some of my aunts and uncles are great, but the others, not so much. Especially my grandmother on my dad's side. My whole life I always felt like we were never good enough and could never live up to her standards. I remember as a little girl walking into her home and seeing pictures of all my cousins on her walls but almost none of Chris and me."

Her expression looks pained as she describes walking into her grandparent's house, and he instantly wants to pull her into his arms and not only protect the woman she is now but the little girl she was back then.

"Oh there would be a picture, but it was a small, two-by-two image of us tucked away into the corner of another frame that already held a big picture of my cousins. I always wondered why she never loved us like the others. She takes a shuddering breath before continuing.

"I was only twelve at the time we immigrated to Canada from South Africa so I never got answers to why she hated us so much, but that feeling of not being wanted didn't go away. When I started school in Toronto the bullying started, and I just felt this crushing weight on my chest, like no matter what I did I just couldn't breathe. Until one day . . ." She trails off, and her eyes glaze over with all the memories.

"Dani, what happened?"

Her eyes are still glazed over when she lifts her hands and turns them over like whatever is in her head is appearing on both of her wrists.

Faded scars still decorate her inner arms but they're less visible now.

"One day I was getting out of the shower and I guess my dad had forgotten to put away his shaving stuff that morning. I found a brand new pack of blades on the counter. It was so tempting, you know? I felt like there was so much pressure building up inside of me and I figured just one little drag of the blade would release some of the pressure and I could breathe again."

She looks up at him with tears streaming down her face, and he stops breathing in that moment.

"And I was right, but then it became almost like an addiction. And then the physical pain was so much better than the emotional pain. I know it sounds fucked up. What kind of thirteen- or fourteen-year-old does that?"

"Dani—"

She doesn't let him finish his sentence as she hurriedly wipes away her tears and turns to face him.

"Anyway, I met Adam a couple months after high school

graduation, we were friends for a little while before we started dating, and for a time he made me forget about the cutting. I started to feel somewhat normal after a few months." She hesitates and looks up at him. "Are you sure you want to hear this?"

He reaches out and takes her small hands in his larger ones squeezing them reassuringly. "Yes, I do."

"For a few months Adam made me forget about how fucked up I was but then he started bringing these friends around every night after work, and they would do drugs and drink in our apartment. They always invited me to join them, and one day I did.

At first all Adam and I would do was smoke a joint or two and have a few beers, but then he started doing cocaine with them and joking that it was okay, he could stop doing it if he wanted to. But he'd just do more of it and then he started drinking more. When he drank more he'd become . . ." Her voice trails off.

"He'd become?"

"He'd become violent: yelling, screaming, and throwing things."

"Did he ever hit you, Dani?"

"Not until a year into our relationship. One night he came home really late, like two or three in the morning. I'd waited up for him, and when he got home he smelled like booze and smoke and another woman's perfume. I confronted him about it. He got so mad, he started yelling at me so I walked out of the room. I didn't get past the door before he yanked my arm and hit me across the face. That was the first time he'd ever laid a hand on me but it wasn't the last. There were many more very similar nights like that one."

He can feel his heart rate pick up speed but he wills himself to stay calm because the last thing he wants is to lose his cool in front of her. But, damn it, he prays he doesn't run in to that bastard.

He wants to protect this woman with every fiber of his being. She's the strongest person he knows.

"One night I couldn't take it anymore so I messaged Kat and Alice and told them I had to get out. I guess you know them as Nicole and Jessica. They argued they wanted to come with me, and they did. That's the real reason why we moved out here. Adam and I were together for close to two years."

She's curled up in a ball with his arms around her. She feels so drained she doesn't think she could move right now even if she wanted to. "I changed my name and dyed my hair dark. Kat and

Alice changed their names and appearances too."

Their wineglasses are sitting half full on the coffee table, and he's breathing really heavily. There were a few times while she was telling him about her past that he drew her closer to him and refused to let go.

She knew then it was hard for him to hear parts of her story. Especially the parts about Adam and the abuse.

"Christ, I'm so sorry Dani."

She looks up at him expecting to see pity in his eyes but all she sees is concern and awe.

"You have nothing to be sorry for, Parker. You weren't there. You had nothing to do with all the shit I went through. I wish I had been strong enough to not have had to go through any of it."

"You're stronger than you give yourself credit for."

She shakes her head and moves to get out of his arms, but they just tighten more around her when he brings her closer.

"You overcame all of it. You fought through everything and you're here today because of that."

She sighs. "I guess." God, if only he knew how much she still struggles to keep the darkness away every day.

He doesn't know though. He doesn't know some nights she still cries herself to sleep while he sleeps next to her. He doesn't know the daily struggle she faces when she opens the bathroom cabinets and sees his razors. She won't ever go back to that kind of release though. She can't.

"What was your name?" he asks curiously.

"Ashley Martens."

"What made you choose Gilbert?"

She smiles shyly. "I kind of had a thing for Brantley Gilbert."

"The country singer?"

She nods. "The one and only."

"You're not worthless by the way. You're beautiful and you're worthy, and I know that wasn't an easy thing for you tell me but I'm glad you did."

"It wasn't. I'm just glad I'm here and he's back in Ontario. He can't hurt me anymore."

He presses a soft kiss to her lips before pulling away

"I'm sorry I lied to you. I wanted to tell you but I was so scared. I still am. I keep thinking that Adam's going to randomly pop up out of nowhere. I have nightmares where I come home, and he's there waiting for me."

He brings her hand up to his lips and places a quick kiss on it, "He won't touch you. I swear on my life I'll protect you from him and anyone else who tries to harm you."

She snuggles more into his side, relieved she was finally able to tell him everything and he's still here.

"Come on. It's your turn to pick the movie, and I'll order the pizza." He pulls her up from the couch with him.

He wasn't expecting all of that when Ashley started telling him about her past. He's still ramped up from it while they sit on the couch watching *The Expendables*.

He was shocked when she told him it was one of her favourite movies. He was even more shocked when she said she loved it because of all the "blow shit up" parts. Yeah, those were her exact words. The woman was after his own heart.

He's not paying attention to the movie though. His brain is still trying to process everything she just told him.

Any man that raises a hand to a woman isn't a man at all in his eyes. Adam's a fucking coward. Parker should call Jay and see if he can still charge the fucker with something. If anyone can find anything about anyone, it's Jay. When Ash gets up to pop more popcorn he shoots off a message.

Parker: Hey, got something to talk to you about. It's important but not tonight

Jay: Mike and I are heading to Brandt's tomorrow after work.

Parker: Count me in.

He makes his way to Jay and Mike's booth in the back and notices the pub is surprisingly slow for after five on a weeknight. Not even a second after he slides into the booth the server is there asking to take their order. All three of them order whatever beer is on tap and several pounds of wings.

"So what's so important?" Jay asks

"We've got an issue," he says.

"What kind of issue?" Mike asks, taking a sip of the beer the server just handed him.

"Dani's ex is an abusive son of a bitch."

"Shit, she finally opened up about her past, huh? What'd the fucker do?" Mike asks

"Beat her to a bloody pulp. Apparently the piece of shit was big into controlling her and using his fists to do it." Parker's hand tightens around his beer glasses until his knuckles are turning white

He still can't think about it without feeling rage boil up inside of him. When he looks at Jay and Mike sitting across from him he knows they're feeling it to, but they're probably not expecting the bomb he's about to drop.

"That's not all. He's the vic's husband."

"How do you figure that?" Mike asks.

"Her ex's name is Adam White. He's also listed as the spouse in the vic's file."

"Shit," Jay says.

"Does she know?" Mike inquires.

"No, I don't think so and I didn't tell her."

"Are you going to tell her?" Jay asks.

"I don't know."

CHAPTER FOURTEEN

She hears her phone ringing somewhere in the distance but she ignores it. This dream is just getting good, and she doesn't want it to end. Parker's doing very dirty things to her body, and she likes it a lot. She tries to force herself back to the dream, but the damn ringing won't stop.

She fumbles blindly around her nightstand trying to locate her phone.

"Hello?" she forces out, her voice groggy with sleep.

"Ash?" Her brother's voice sounds panicked.

She sits up, instantly alert, clicking on the bedroom light. "Chris? What's wrong?"

"Ash, it's Dad . . ." His voice hitches, but he doesn't go on.

"What about Dad? Chris, what's going on?"

"Dad . . . had a heart attack tonight. He . . . he didn't make it." She can hear Chris sobbing into the phone now.

Dear God, please, no. She just talked to her dad earlier in the day. They were laughing while planning her trip home this summer, and their family vacation next year. He was laughing and happy and he was alive.

"Ash?"

"I'm still here." She tries to wipe away the tears, but they're coming faster than she can keep up with. "Where are you? Where's Mom?" Even though her parents had been divorced for a few years they still cared deeply for each other.

"She's here. We're still at the hospital."

"Put her on." She hears rustling before her mom's voice comes through the phone.

"Hello? Ashley?"

"Mom . . ." She can't keep back the sobs that rack her body anymore. She'd had to be strong for her brother but she can't hold it back for her mom.

"I'm here, Ashley." Her mom's voice cracks but she can tell she's trying to keep it together for her and Chris.

"I'm coming home. I want to come home."

"Ashley, you have a thesis to finish right now. Why don't you wait until we have the funeral figured out and come home then?"

"No," she replies forcefully and she instantly regrets it. "I'm coming home now and I'll help with the funeral arrangements. I'll book a ticket right now and be there tomorrow."

Her mom sighs into the phone. "Okay. Message me your flight info and I'll pick you up at the airport."

"Okay. I love you."

"I love you too, Ashley," her mom says before the line goes dead.

It's been so long since she's been back home. She came home the first Christmas after she left for school, but with the flights being so expensive she hadn't had a chance to get back here.

However, this was not the way she pictured she'd be coming home.

Dad had a heart attack tonight. He . . . he didn't make it. Her life changed with that one phone call. She couldn't even lean on Parker right now because it felt like they'd drifted apart ever since she told him about her past. He claimed he just couldn't get the time away from the team right now; they were just too busy.

They'd caught a new homicide case the other week, and recently he's had to put in double hours at the station, helping the Organized Crime Unit crack a couple cases they were working on.

She understood. She did. Being a member of the ERT came with a lot of responsibilities, but she didn't think she was making a big request.

All she wanted was at least one night a week where it was just the two of them. One night when they could reconnect as a couple. She didn't think that was too much to ask.

CHAPTER FIFTEEN

"What do you mean you can't find him, Jay?" Parker's pacing his office now like a caged animal.

This can't be happening. Jay's been searching for Adam for a week now and no leads. Where did the fucker disappear to?

"We've searched everywhere, man, and nothing. The guy's a fucking ghost. He put in for leave from work. The Ontario Provincial Police couldn't find him either."

"What about his debit card? Credit cards? Cell phone?"

"Nothing new has shown up since April."

"Three months? Fuck!"

"We'll keep searching, Parker, but it's not looking good."

He takes a deep breath and lets it out. He still has a briefing with the Organized Crime unit before he can call it a day. "Yeah, thanks, man. I appreciate it."

"How's Dani doing?"

"I don't know. I've barely been home. If I see her I'm going to spill about asking you to look into Adam, she'll tell me to stop and let it go. But I can't let it go, Jay. This guy hurt her badly, and on top of that he's the number one suspect in our investigation."

"We'll catch him, but you need to talk to her."

"I know. I've been working doubles. The Organized Crime Unit needed some backup on a few cases."

Jay chuckles on the other end of the line. "That sucks. Sorry man."

"Let's hope she doesn't fucking hate me after this."

"She might if you don't tell her the truth."

His phone beeps with an incoming call. When he looks down at it he sees it's not a number he recognizes. He ends the call with Jay and immediately answers the incoming call.

"Collins."

"Parker, it's Jess."

"Hey, Jess. What can I help you with?"

"Look, I'm just going to cut to the chase. I'm not sure what game you're playing with my best friend and right now I don't care. She needs you."

"I'm not playing games with her, Jess, work has been busy. Is she okay?"

"No. Her dad passed away early this morning. She just got the phone call."

His breath leaves him as he stumbles back into his leather office chair. "I'm on my way to your place right now."

"She's not there, Parker—"

"Where are you? I'll come get her."

"Parker, she's not here either—"

"Damn it, Jessica! Where is she?"

"Look, asshole, I didn't have to call you and tell you, but she really likes you, and I have a feeling you might love her, so you should be there for her right now. I put her on a plane home about ten minutes ago. There's another flight leaving for Toronto in two hours—"

He didn't need to hear the rest of what Jess was saying. He hangs up and grabs his keys before hauling ass out to the car and to the airport. He didn't need his passport to fly within the country, and he could buy clothes once he got there, but his girl needed him. He had a lot of groveling to do.

. . . and I have a feeling you might love her . . .

Jessica's words play like a broken record in his head while he sits in his seat waiting for the plane to take off.

Nausea rolls through his stomach, and something akin to heartburn grips his chest. He doesn't do love.

It's not a word he includes in his vocabulary. Does he believe in love? Sure, he does. But does he love her? Even if he did, he wouldn't be able to tell. He's never been in love nor has he said those three little words to anyone. He may have never been in love but he also doesn't believe in flinging those words around to just anyone.

CHAPTER SIXTEEN

"Ash, can you get the door!" Chris yells from the living room where he's been playing that damn PS3 game ever since she got to their dad's house earlier this morning. He's only stopped to scarf down a couple slices of pizza and go to the bathroom. She has no idea how he can just sit in front of the TV for eight hours straight like that.

Shaking her head, she goes to answer the front door but she's not prepared to see Parker on the other side.

"What are you doing here?"

"Jess told me what happened."

She sighs and leans her head against the propped open door.

Of course she did.

"You didn't need to come out here."

"Why didn't you call me? I would've come with you, Danielle. You didn't have to do this by yourself."

"Would you have? Because lately it seems like you live at the station. I haven't had a conservation with you that wasn't over text in several days, Parker. And I'm not doing it by myself. Chris and my mom are helping where they can."

Although, they're really not. Her brother, Chris, is too young to help with all the legal stuff.

"Damn it, Danielle, yes, I would've been there. You're more important than work. There'll always be other ERT members who can take over for me, but there's only one you."

She wants to believe him when he says he would've been there, she really did, but history has a way of repeating itself.

She straightens up from leaning on the door frame and steps outside, closing the door behind her.

"If there'll always be other team members to take over for you then where were they these last few days?"

Fuck, she knows she sounds like a whiny bitch but she needs to know what she did to make him avoid her.

He runs a hand through his hair and looks at her with regret in his eyes, and her stomach instantly falls. "Do we have to do this right here? Let's go grab a coffee and talk."

"If you're breaking up with me, you could've saved yourself a plane ticket and just texted me."

"What? I'm not breaking up with you, Danielle."

But she's not buying it. She crosses her arms over her chest and narrows her eyes at him. Trying not to think about how hot he looks in his fitted, navy blue dress pants and white, button-up shirt.

He's not wearing a jacket, and his sleeves are rolled up to his elbows. The top two buttons of his shirt are undone, exposing a bit of the eagle tattoo on his chest.

Despite the four hours spent on a plane and the hour drive from the airport he still looks perfectly put together.

"Shit. Okay, looks like we're doing this here." He runs a hand through his hair again and stuffs them both inside the front pockets of his pants. "I didn't have to pick up all those other cases but I did. I picked them up because I couldn't stand to lie to you and I figured if I spent most of my time at the station working on other cases then I wouldn't have to."

"Lie to me about what?"

"I asked Jay to see if he could track down Adam." He looks at her regretfully.

"What? Why would you do that?" Her arms drop to her side, and her back straightens as her voice rises in volume.

"Because I couldn't stand what he'd done to you, and he needs to pay."

"So you go track down my abusive ex, and what? Hope I don't find out? Hope it doesn't drag all those painful memories back up? What was your goal in this, Parker? Please, help me understand what you were thinking when you asked Jay to go digging up my past." Her face flushes red with anger.

"I was thinking that son of a bitch needs to pay for what he did to you! That I wanted to find him before he found you!"

They're both yelling now but neither of them seems to care. She feels sick and she can't believe he'd go behind her back and do that.

She gets where he's coming from but all she wanted was for her past to stay buried in the past. She can't think about Adam right now. Not with what's happened with her dad.

His funeral being only days away, everything has fallen on her: making the plans, notifying his work and his landlord, and taking care of his estate.

She sighs, feeling defeated. She doesn't want to fight with him. She's glad he's here but she just needs him to be there for her right now.

"I'm not some helpless thing, Parker. I don't need you to fight my battles for me."

He pulls her into a hug and kisses her forehead. "I know and I'm sorry. I'm sorry for keeping this from you and making you feel like I abandoned you."

She wraps her arms around his waist and grasps his shirt at his back praying he doesn't let go and buries her face in the crook of his neck, inhaling him in. She's missed this.

"Did you find him?"

He sighs and gently nudges her chin up with his finger until she's looking up at him. "Jay's still looking, but so far no hits have come up. But if anyone can find him, it's Jay. He can't hide forever."

She looks down, noticing for the first time he doesn't have any luggage with him. When she looks back up at him with a raised eyebrow there's a grin on his face. "No bags?"

"I was in my office when Jess called. I went straight to the airport and got the first plane out. Packing wasn't high on my list."

Shaking her head, she laughs and leads him inside the house, "Come on, Romeo, it's been a long day, and I'm tired. We'll go get you clothes tomorrow when the mall opens."

After Ash and Parker got back from shopping for clothes and picking out a suit for the funeral tomorrow, he decided to spend some time getting to know Chris.

She'd told him Chris was the one who heard their dad call out in the middle of the night and who realized he was having a heart attack. He stayed with him while the ambulance was on its way.

He couldn't even begin to imagine how Chris must be feeling after having to watch his dad die in his arms and not being able to do anything. That would wreck anyone, but the kid's only sixteen.

"Bravo team, go left. Alpha team, go right," Chris says into his head set.

Parker has no idea what game they're playing so he's just following Chris's lead. It goes to show how often Parker got to just chill and hang out on his couch and play video games.

The last time he picked up a controller he was probably

seventeen and in his junior year of high school. There was never enough time to play games after that.

"Parker, watch your six!" Chris yells at him right before the screen goes red and they lose the game.

"Shit. Sorry man."

"No worries. I was due for a lunch break anyways. I'm fucking starving!"

"I ordered a pizza for you guys," Ashley says walking into the living room.

"Sweet. Thanks, sis."

"You're welcome, Chris."

She walks over to Parker and places a kiss on his cheek. He notices, not for the first time, how beautiful she is. This woman has the strength of steel. It takes an amazing amount of courage to go through what she went through and come out whole on the other side.

"I'm going to the funeral home to drop off the final payment."

"Want me to come with you?"

"Nah, looks like you guys are really into your game, and I won't be long."

Chris hands him back the controller and starts another game. He tries not to fuck it up this time, and their team finally completes their mission.

Her phone rings as she's walking back to her car.

One more day and then she'll never have to visit the funeral home again. At least for a while anyway. Everyone is just way too nice there. Almost overly nice. Always asking her how she's doing. Letting her know that if she needs anything, they offer a wide range of services, including grief counselling.

Yeah, no thanks.

"Hello?" she says settling into the driver's seat of her VW Jetta.

"Miss Ashley Martens?" the deep voice on the other side asks.

Her blood runs cold, nobody from her new life knows her real name. No one except Parker and her two best friends but neither of them would ever give out that information.

"Yes?" she hesitantly answers.

"I'm constable Smith from the OPP. Would you and your

brother be able to come down to the station today. It's about your dad."

"I don't understand. My dad's funeral is tomorrow."

"I understand that and I'm sorry for your loss, but it's important that the both of you come in. Neither of you are in trouble, we just have a couple questions in regards to your dad's death."

She reluctantly agrees to meet Constable Smith at the station with Chris in a couple hours.

"Constable Smith?" Parker asks when they approach his desk.

"Yes. And you are?" The burly man looks up from the stack of papers on his desk.

"I'm Parker Collins. I'm part of the RCMP in BC. This is Ashley and Chris Martens." He gestures behind them.

"Ms. Martens. Mr. Martens," Constable Smith says, standing up from his desk and shaking each of their hands. "Please have a seat."

Ashley and Chris sit in the two chairs provided in front of his desk with Parker preferring to stand behind Ashley with a reassuring hand on her shoulder.

"Do you know if your dad was taking potassium for any reason?" Constable Smith asks from behind his desk.

Parker looks at her and Chris, they both shake their heads no. As far as she knew her dad wasn't taking any medication or vitamins. He was extremely healthy. He ran every morning and never missed a squash tournament.

"Why do you ask?" she questions.

"The lab work showed large amounts of potassium in your dad's blood."

"I thought you said he died of a heart attack," Chris says, confused.

Constable Smith nods. "Large amounts of potassium like this can cause cardiac arrest. But we never see these amounts in someone taking it as a daily supplement. These levels are even high for an overdose."

"I'm sorry, but what are you saying?" Parker demands.

"I'm saying it looks like there might be foul play involved in their dad's death."

"You think someone killed him?" she questions.

"It's possible." Smith looks to Chris, "Was your dad acting strangely at all over the past few days?"

"I'm not sure. We had an away game this week. I was gone for two nights. I found him the night I got back."

"Game?"

"Football. I'm a running back for our high school team," Chris says.

Constable Smith jots down notes in a file and then shuts it. "I apologize for having to bring all this up again, but we wanted to make sure all our bases were covered."

He stands and offers his hand to her, Chris, and then Parker. "If anything new comes up we'll let you know right away."

She, Parker, and Chris leave the station, their heads are spinning with the new information they just received.

The Ontario Provincial Police suspect foul play in their dad's death but they didn't elaborate as to a possible motive.

"I'll get my team to look into it," Parker reassures her, but she just nods, still not entirely sure what just happened. Who would want to murder her dad?

CHAPTER SEVENTEEN

There's a small gathering at the funeral the next day. Ashley had decided to not have it open to the public, just family or by invite only. That didn't; however, stop their estranged great-aunt from crashing the funeral, who then proceeds to pull her aside to ask if she could give Ashley's dad's eulogy.

Ashley was really glad when Parker intervened, told her aunt politely no her aunt couldn't give the eulogy and then dragged Ashley away before she gave her estranged aunt a piece of her mind—impolitely.

Her aunt had only ever met her dad once in his life so for her to have the balls to come up to her and ask her was not sitting well with Ashley. She shouldn't have shown up in the first place.

He wraps an arm around her shoulders and leads her into one of the private rooms at the back of the funeral home. He's trying to comfort her the best he can, but she's having a tough time coming to terms with her dad's sudden death.

When he closes the door behind them, she pushes his arm away and walks further into the room. Her shoulders heaving with each struggle of breath. "I can't believe he's really gone." She sobs.

When people tell her it'll get better, that it gets easier, she wants to scream. How is something that hurts this much, that literally makes her feel like her heart is breaking, supposed to get better?

"Danielle—"

"He'll never walk me down the aisle, Parker. He'll never see me get married or have kids."

She moves to the window and watches as rain starts gently falling on this July day. He walks up behind her, wrapping his big arms around her.

Her dad wasn't poor but he wasn't a rich man either, and that never stopped him from making sure his children were taken care of. He didn't mind sacrificing if it meant his kids were happy. Her mom didn't either.

She may be a grown adult but she still needs her dad. She needs her best friend back. And right now she doesn't care if God has a better plan. She really doesn't.

Chris's words are the only things that penetrate her thoughts as she sits in the pew of the funeral home.

"When a man raises a man, a bond is made. A father-son relationship is a connection that will never be torn apart, not by death, not by separation. When the person's gone the love still lingers. It hurts to let that soul slip through our fingers, but as I grow older I start to realize I'm my father's son, and no good deed goes undone. Rest in peace, Dad. We love you."

"So tell me the truth Dani. How are you really doing?" he asks, still keeping his eyes on the stars.

When everyone left after the funeral, Parker and Ashley decided to drive down to the lake and take a walk along the boardwalk.

This was always her favourite thing to do when she'd had a long or stressful day.

An audible sigh escapes her lips.

How am I doing?

The last couple days felt like her body was on autopilot. It had felt like she was in limbo, and everything was just moving around her. She was standing still, but life for everyone else kept going forward. Didn't they know? Didn't they care that her father was just killed?

Before the funeral, everything felt like a bad joke someone was playing on her. But it wasn't, she'd seen him lying there on the stainless steel table with a white cloth covering everything but his face. Motionless. Not breathing.

She'd wanted him to move, to get up from the table, to walk over to her, hug her, and to tell her it was a mistake, that he wasn't dead.

During the funeral was when everything started to go by in a blur: the people, the minister, the service. None of it felt real.

She sits up, suddenly very focused on the waves crashing on the beach.

She didn't know how to put it all into words he or anyone would understand.

"Honestly?" She takes a deep breath trying to organize her thoughts. "I don't know how I'm doing. I'm fine until somebody mentions his name or I see a picture of him or a memory invades my head."

Tears are threatening to spill but she wills them back. He sits up and inches closer to her.

"I feel almost guilty. I mean he was my father but at times I find myself forgetting him; forgetting his face, forgetting his laugh, his voice, his hug. Other times I still expect to see him come home around dinner time. One day I caught myself wanting to dial his number and talk to him."

A tear escapes and the barricade that had been holding them back breaks, the tears flowing freely now.

"Danielle—" he starts but decides against it.

Danielle, what? What could he even say to that? He'd never lost a parent so he didn't know exactly what she was going through. He could imagine the war of emotions going on inside of her but he couldn't know exactly.

What does one say to someone who's lost a parent? There was only one thing he could do for her and that was to make sure she knew he'd always be there ready to listen with open arms if she ever needed it.

"I don't know if there's anything I can say or do that would take away some of the hurt you're feeling but what I can do is promise to always be here to lend an ear." Reaching an arm around her shoulders he pulls her closer into him. "I've been told I have a knack for listening to people vent."

She smiles through her tears. "Thanks, but you know me. I'm a suffer-in-silence sort of girl."

"How's Chris handling all of this?"

She shakes her head. "No sixteen-year-old should have to find their parent like that. He pretends he's okay; hiding behind video games and working on his car, but I know he's not. How can he be?"

"Give him time. He'll come around eventually."

"I wish he would just open up to me. We've been best friends practically since he was born. We've always been closer than other siblings, but he won't even talk to me about how he feels. The only time I've seen him cry is at the funeral. I mean, I'm not saying he has to cry but I want to know what he's feeling, what he's going through. I want to help him. I want to be there for him." She sighs and drops her head. "Lately, it just feels like he's shut everyone out."

He rubs his hands up and down her arms. "He probably still needs time to process it all, but you've said it yourself: the two of you are close. So I'm guessing when he's good and ready to talk about it he'll be the one to bring it up. From the little I've seen, Chris seems like he's a private person. He likes to keep things close to the chest. Don't be surprised if he never wants to talk about it, but he'll work through it in his own time and in his own way."

"I just feel guilty." She softly leans her head back onto his shoulder, and he sees fresh tears streaming down her cheeks.

"Why do you feel guilty?"

"Because I wasn't here. I wasn't here when he found our dad dying in his bed. I was across the country. I should have been here."

"Danielle, your dad wanted you to be safe from Adam."

"I know." She looks at him with sadness in her eyes, and at that moment he wants to wrap her up in his arms and protect her from the world. "I wasn't there for Chris and I should've been. No sixteen-year-old should have to watch their parent die."

"You shouldn't have had to see that either."

"No, but I would've preferred it to be me rather than Chris."

"You can't protect him forever, Danielle."

"I get it. I do. But he'll always be my baby brother, and I'll always want to protect him from the darkness of this world."

"Spoken from experience."

"Yeah, sorry about that. I didn't mean to dump all that shit on you."

"I like that you did. I just wish you hadn't had to go through all that shit in your past. And if I ever cross paths with Adam I'll kill him."

She laughs softly, and it's the most amazing sound he's heard all week. Standing up he brushes the sand off his jeans before offering her his hand and helping her up.

"Come on, let's go get some ice cream. Double fudge cookie dough?"

"A man after my own heart." She grins.

CHAPTER EIGHTEEN

"You should move in," Parker states, caressing her arm as they're relaxing in bed on a late Sunday morning in August with the sun streaming through the open curtains.

With his help she was able to progress through the beginning stages of grief. It has only been a month since the funeral, but during that time she hasn't touched a bottle of Jack or picked up a razor.

It's progress. Two years ago she would've given in to the depression and desire to self-harm. But not this time. This time she was surrounded by people who loved and cared for her and who'd always be there to drag her out if things got dark again.

She has him to partly thank for that. Whenever she found herself starting the downward spiral all she had to do was seek him out, and he would be there with arms wide open, ready to give her whatever she needed. Whether that was just to feel him engulf her in a hug or someone to whom she could vent her frustrations.

The random long-stemmed roses she's found around her apartment and in her car didn't hurt either.

"I should?" She smiles.

He tugs her closer and places a soft kiss on the top of her head. "Just say yes."

"And if I don't?" she asks playfully.

"Then I might just have to tickle you until you do." He laughs.

She pulls back to look at him. "You wouldn't."

He grins and raises an eyebrow in response then flips her onto her back and straddles her legs.

He attacks the most ticklish parts of her sides and under her arms. Before long she's immersed in a fit of laughter so hard she can barely breathe.

"Okay! Okay!"

"Is that a yes?"

"Yes! Just please stop." She laughs.

Parker grins triumphantly, moving back to his side of the bed.

"You don't play fair." She lightheartedly smacks him on his chest.

"Who said anything about fair, babe?"

"Meanie." She sticks her tongue out at him.

His eyes darken. "If you're going to be sticking out your tongue,

Danielle, I can think of better ways to use it."

Heat creeps up her cheeks just as his phone beeps on the bedside table with an incoming message. He picks it up reading the text.

"I gotta go, babe," he states, climbing out of bed and locating his jeans on the bedroom floor.

"What's going on?"

"Looks like they found another body." He places a quick kiss on her lips before pulling a shirt over his head. "I'll call you when I know more."

"Okay."

Parker flashes his badge at the uniformed officer before moving under the yellow tape and walking over to Jay, who's hunched over the naked body of a young female.

Her dark hair is fanned out around her shoulders, her dark eyes widened in shock. Ligature marks are visible on her wrists and ankles.

"What do we have?"

"Twenty-five-year-old female. Driver's license says Ashleigh Berg. Suspected sexual assault, but we won't know for sure until the coroner does an autopsy."

"Any witnesses?" He looks around the deserted parking lot of the visitor's centre.

"None." Jay straightens up from the body and inclines his head towards a sign in the distance. "You see what I see?"

"The Alberta border," Parker states.

"This was just the dump site."

"You think she was killed over the border?"

Jay hands him the evidence bag containing the victim's driver's license. "The address on her driver's license is an Alberta one."

"Gentlemen."

Parker and Jay nod their greeting as the coroner approaches them.

"Bryan, tell me you can give me a time or cause of death," Jay begs.

"Well," Bryan starts, bending down and examining the body, "the body is still in rigor mortis. So I'd say she's been dead for less than thirty-six hours. As for the cause of death, I won't have an answer for you until I can examine her more fully."

"Sergeant!" a uniformed officer yells from across the parking lot.

"Call us as soon you have something, Doc," Parker says before turning and heading back towards the parking lot.

When they catch up to the officer their gazes follow the direction he's pointing to.

"Tire tracks," Parker states.

"This is a visitor's centre off the main highway coming into B.C. There could be lots of tire tracks in this parking lot," Jay states.

"Centre's been closed for a number of years There's no reason for anyone to stop here with a diner about five more minutes down the road," the officer informs them.

"Get forensics and get a casting of the tire track," Parker demands.

"I can't believe you're moving in with him," Kat says, taping another box closed.

"I know. Never thought I'd be doing it again." she walks around Kat to place another box by the door so the guys can take it down to the truck.

"It'll be weird not having you here." Alice places another box on top of the one Ashley put down.

"It's not like I'm moving far. When Parker goes over to Mike's to watch the game I expect you ladies to be ready for hours of *Criminal Minds* and wine."

"Deal." Kat and Alice laugh.

"I'll also be taking full advantage of that pool," Alice adds.

"Definitely," Kat agrees.

"Is this the last of it?" Parker asks, walking through the front door.

All three women turn as him, Mike, and Jay lift the three boxes by the door.

"Yes, thank you, guys."

"I seriously need to get me one of those." Alice hooks her thumb over her shoulder, looking back at Ashley.

Ashley laughs, "Well two of them are single." She bumps shoulders with Alice.

Kat chokes and starts coughing while folding the rest of Ashley's clothes.

"You okay, Kat?" Ashley and Alice look worriedly at her.

"Yeah, fine."

When they get the truck unloaded and Ashley's boxes put in their respective rooms the six of them plop down on Parker's black, leather, L-shaped couch, each with their own beer.

"Gotcha's?" Mike asks from his seat on the recliner.

"I'm in," Alice answers enthusiastically.

Kat nods. "Me too."

Parker and Ashley exchange a knowing look before he turns his head to Mike. "I think we're going to call it a night."

Mike groans. "You already sound like an old, married couple."

"Come on, babe," Jay says, offering his hand for Kat to help her up off the couch.

Ashley's eyebrow raises at the endearment.

"Babe?" Ashley whispers into Kat's ear when they're hugging goodbye at the front door.

Kat just shrugs and grins before following the other three out of the door.

"What was that about?" he asks, coming up behind Ashley and slipping his arms around her belly.

"I'm not entirely sure."

CHAPTER NINETEEN

Hearing the front door open and close she grabs her other stiletto and tries to put it on while hoping out of the downstairs bathroom to greet Parker.

"Hey, I thought I was meeting you at the restaurant."

"Hello, Ashley."

Her body instantly freezes at that voice and she slowly lifts her head, praying he's not really standing in front her right now.

She has to be dreaming. There's no way he's here in BC. At any moment her alarm is going to go off and she'll wake up alone in the bed she shares with Parker.

But when her eyes meet the midnight ones of the man standing at the front door she knows this isn't a dream.

"Adam? What are you doing here? How did you—"

"I told you I'd have you again, Ashley," Adam says as he reaches behind him and turns the lock in the door, then the dead bolt. "And I always get what I want."

The way he says her name has the hair on the back of her neck standing up, and her blood pumping in fear.

Memories of lying on the living room floor of their apartment while Adam landed kick after kick to her ribs invade her head, and she starts shaking. Her eyes glance over to the alarm box by the door.

When she moved into Parker's house, he and Jay insisted they get the thing installed, especially because Jay hadn't been able to track down Adam's whereabouts.

Jay had added a feature where if a certain button was pressed on the keypad or in the app on her phone, it would send an emergency SOS signal to his and Parker's cell phones. Installing it was a good idea in practice but right now it's not coming in handy since she'd forgotten to reset it after entering the house earlier.

"You've been a bad girl, Ashley," Adam says, stalking closer to her. "Pretending with that other man. But I know you, Ashley."

He successfully backs her into the far wall of the living room, cutting off her only exit. The stench of stale whiskey and cigarettes coming off him is enough to make her gag.

"You're drunk."

"I'm always drunk, Ashley. Ever since you ran away from me."

"You put me in the hospital the same night you got engaged, or did you forget?" She knows she's playing with fire right now and she should be fucking scared of this monster but she's not. She's surprisingly calm. She won't allow him to hurt her anymore. She's spent the majority of the last couple years in fear of this man and she refuses to let him have that much power over her now. She refuses to be a fucking toy he plays with. "I'm not scared of you—"

Adam's eyes are completely cold when he smirks and wraps his hand around her neck, slamming her back into the wall. She can feel the warmth of his breath on her cheek when he leans in.

"You should be," he whispers lightly, dragging his nose up her jaw and licking her bottom lip.

Instinctively she moves her head to the side but immediately his hand leaves her neck, grabs her face, and moves it back so she's facing him once again. "You're going to regret ever walking away from me, *Danielle*. You're mine. And I don't like sharing what's mine."

"I'm not yours, Adam." She stares at him defiantly. "I'm not some possession. Now, let me go." She pushes against his chest.

"I've watched you with him."

He's still leaning into her with his one hand propped up on the wall, blocking her in while his other hand strokes along her collarbone. Goose bumps rake down her body, not out of desire but fear.

She knows what Adam's capable of and as much as she's told herself she won't show any fear of this man, her body is betraying her. All she wants to do is run away screaming but she can't.

His fingers continue to stroke lightly up and down her collarbone. She shrinks back at the touch. It doesn't matter that two years ago she used to crave that same touch. But it's not the same. Back then it was her drug of choice ; she craved it. She needed it to be able to forget about the issues that were constantly plaguing her.

But now, now it was underlined with something sinister and she wanted to recoil in disgust.

"He seems quite fond of you. It's too bad he won't get to enjoy you for much longer."

His hand skims lightly down her arm, and she feels a small prick on the inside of her elbow. She looks down just in time to see him placing a needle back in his jacket pocket.

Her head starts to feel heavy, her arms and legs numb. He catches her and picks her up before her body can hit the floor. Panic races through her.

"Don't worry, the paralysis is only temporary. If I wanted to kill you, Ashley, you'd be dead already. You'll start to gain some control back in about twenty-five to thirty minutes."

Adam gently lays her down on the couch and covers her with a blanket. "You see, Ashley. This was just to prove you can't run from me. You might be able to change your name and your appearance, but you'll never be able to hide. I'll always find you."

Adam smirks and then gets up, moving out of sight, but she can hear him walking around the kitchen then towards the front door before his footsteps are moving back to the kitchen.

Before long his face appears above her, and his hand goes back to its assault on her collarbone before roaming down to her breasts. She inwardly cringes, wishing she could move but nothing happens when she tries wiggling her fingers for what feels like the fiftieth time.

"I think I'm going to rather enjoy watching that boy toy of yours die," Adam says before his face and hand disappear. "I'll let you enjoy what little freedom you have left because I'm coming back for you, Ashley, and you'll be mine. He won't be able to save you."

Tears steak down the sides of her face as she hears the front door open and click shut. Adam's words play on repeat as she lies on the couch, staring up at the ceiling, unable to move.

She has no idea what Adam has planned for either of them, but his words echo in her head.

He won't be able to save you . . .

When the drug has worn off enough for her to move her arms and turn her head a bit, she tries to reach for her phone on the floor beside the couch, but something on the coffee table catches her eye.

Sitting in a vase filled with water is a single red rose. It looks exactly like the ones she's found in her condo and on her car. Her blood runs cold.

Adam.

Adam left all those roses.

CHAPTER TWENTY

"Dani! Danielle!" Parker yells as soon as he pushes open the front door and scans the entry into the living room.

When she didn't show up at the restaurant on time he figured she'd been held up at her office on campus grading freshman papers, but when twenty minutes passed by without a text or phone call he started to worry.

Twenty minutes turned into forty, and he knew something wasn't right. Dani always called or texted if she was going to be even five minutes late.

Body raking sobs sound from the kitchen, and he runs in that direction without hesitation. She's sitting on the kitchen floor with her back pressed to the cupboards, her knees drawn up to her body. Her arms are wrapped around her legs with her forehead resting on her knees. A garbage can filled with red roses sits next to her.

"Dani?"

Her cheeks are tear stained, and her black mascara is running down her face when she lifts her head at his voice. "It was Adam."

His stomach drops, and dread fills him. His eyes quickly scan her from top to bottom looking for any injuries, but there are none. "What was?"

She points to the garbage can filled to the brim with roses, some of which look like they've been dried. "I thought it was you. I thought you were the one leaving a single, red rose in random places where you knew I'd find them that's why I kept them. But it wasn't you; it was Adam."

"Are you okay? Did he hurt you?"

She sobs even harder, her entire body shaking from the intensity. "He drugged me."

He shrugs out of his suit jacket and places it on the kitchen counter, then he sits down next to her and pulls her into his arms.

"He was here when I was getting ready to go meet you at the restaurant. I thought it was you coming through the door, like maybe you forgot your wallet or something, but when I came out of the downstairs bathroom Adam was here."

"Did he touch you? What did he want?"

She's crying hysterically now and throws her arms around him in a steel-like grip. He swears if Adam laid a hand on his girl it'll be his last day with that hand.

"Sh, it's okay, babe." He pulls her closer into him and rubs her back.

She mumbles something in response, but her face is buried in his shoulder, and he can't make out a word she's saying.

"What was that?"

"It's not okay, Parker. He said he's going to kill you."

Gently placing his hands on either side of her face, he tries to dab at some of her tears, but they're flowing faster than he can wipe them away, so instead he searches her green eyes with his blue ones. "He's not going to kill me, Dani. He was trying to scare you."

She hiccups, and he thinks it must be the cutest thing he's heard all day until she opens her mouth and lets out a string of swear words.

Hearing her curse is pretty amusing too. On the outside she looks like an innocent twenty-four-year-old, but then she's got a mouth like a sailor.

"Well it fucking worked! That sick, twisted son of a bitch!"

"Where were the roses?"

"The first one was left in my condo the day we had our first date. The second one was in one of the lecture halls I TA in. After that I found them in my car, in my office on campus, in the labs I'd teach. More recently I've found them on my driver's seat, outside our front door, and . . ."

"Where else, Danielle?"

"Our bed." She turns abruptly in his arms. "Oh, God, Parker! He's been in this house when we weren't home!"

He wraps his arms around her more securely and tries to reassure her. "I'm calling the team in. He won't be able to touch you again."

Parker finally gets her calmed down and soaking in a hot bath with lush bath bombs and a full glass of her favourite white wine when his phone rings.

"Jay?"

"He's in town, Parker."

"I know. He was in our house. Danielle thought it was me coming through the front door."

"Shit! Did he hurt her?"

"I didn't see any bruising. He shook her up pretty good, spewed some shit about wanting to kill me."

"You don't believe he's capable of that?"

"I think he wanted to scare her and did a pretty good job of it."

"If he has access to your house we need to bring the team in on this, Parker."

"Agreed, but I'm not leaving Danielle alone right now." Parker sighs. "Shit, there's only one way this is going to go down."

"Have you told her about the multiple homicides?"

"Not yet, we'll have to tell her today. But I know her, she'll blame herself first and then she'll want in on the case."

"Roger that."

Now comes the hard part.

CHAPTER-TWENTY-ONE

There are ten men in the living room, all of them in tactical gear. What the actual fuck is going on?

Ashley came downstairs, relaxed and calm after the amazing bath Parker had put together for her, to find him, Jay, Mike, and seven other deadly looking guys, with their heads bent together in an intense conversation.

Previously he'd come upstairs with another member of the team to take her blood so they could test it for any remnants of the drug Adam had used, but she didn't see him among the men in their dining room.

She doesn't notice her at first, but Bella is coloring in a brand new coloring book on the rug on the living room floor. A huge grin splits her face when she sees Ashley. Bella throws down her pencil crayons, jumps up, and runs over to her with her arms wide.

"Dani!"

"Hey, princess! Whatcha coloring?" She bends down and scoops Bella up in her arms.

"Parker bought me a *Descendants* coloring book."

"He did, did he?"

Bella nods her head enthusiastically.

"Where's your sister?"

"She's in the kitchen making dinner. Can I go back to coloring now?" Bella wiggles in her arms, making Ashley laugh as she puts her down.

"Sure thing, princess. I'll come join you in a bit."

Anne is throwing chopped vegetables into a pot when Ashley walks in the kitchen. "Smells good in here."

"Hey, Dani." Anne grins, pulling her into a hug.

"Hey, Anne. What are you making? My mouth's watering just from the smell." Ashley laughs hugging Anne back.

"Beef stew. It's my specialty."

"Sounds good. I can't wait to try it." Ashley walks around the counter and takes a seat on one of the bar stools while Anne goes back to cooking.

"It shouldn't be too much longer."

Movement catches Ashley's eye and she turns to see the guys leaning over the dining room table with various papers strewn about.

"Thanks, Anne."

"You guys caught a new case?" she asks, walking up next to the men surrounding the dining room table.

The team goes silent and Matt looks from Parker, to Jay, and then to Mike uncertainly.

Parker concedes. "Go ahead. Might as well tell her now. She'll find out soon enough."

Matt nods, clearing his throat. "Multiple homicides. All female. All brunette. All five-five or shorter. All of them killed on the other side of the Alberta border."

Parker slowly hands her the file he's holding, "Jennifer White was the first victim."

"Jennifer White?" she opens the file, but her forehead creases in confusion when she sees the picture of the beautiful, blonde, blue eyed twenty-five-year-old. "I thought you said all the victims were brunettes." She closes the file then hold it up. "She doesn't fit the victim profile."

"No, she doesn't. She's the only one who doesn't," Jay announces.

"But there's a reason for that," Parker adds.

"Which is what?" She glances up at him.

"She was Adam's wife."

Her stomach drops. "What are you saying?"

"We're saying you might want to prepare yourself to have protection wherever you go from now on because Adam has become our primary suspect for these murders," Jay states

"His rental car has been flagged making multiple trips back and forth across the border around the same time their bodies were dumped."

Parker shoots Mike a look to shut him up before he can say anything else, but it doesn't go unnoticed by her.

"What?" She tilts her head and narrows her eyes at him. "What are you not telling me, Parker?"

"We have reason to believe that he's killing to send us a message. To send you a message," Parker says.

"Danielle, all of these women look like you," Jay says apologetically.

She slaps the file down on the table and crosses her arms over her chest. "Maybe it's a coincidence."

"Dani—" Parker starts, but she cuts him off.

"No, Parker. I can't believe Adam is doing this because then it means he actually could make good on this threat to kill you." She inhales deeply then releases her breath. "What makes you think he did all this? Besides the dead wife."

Mike stands up and hands her another file. This one has a picture of a little girl around three years old. Light brown hair hangs in pigtails down her shoulders, and her dark brown eyes are smiling at the camera.

"Shauna White. Adam's younger sister," Mike states before sitting back down.

"How did she die?" she inquires quietly, still staring at the little girl in the picture.

"Official report says she drowned in the family's pool back in 1996," Nick, another member of the team, adds from across the table.

"Why do I feel like there's a but in there?"

"But that's what the unsealed file says. The sealed file says that it was suspected homicide," Nick finishes.

"Inspector Porter was able to get the file unsealed for us," Cole adds.

She looks questionably around the table, hoping one of these men will be able to give her a straight answer,

"Can somebody please explain to me what the hell is going on? Are you saying that Adam killed his three-year-old sister? He was ten at the time. That's insane."

"That's what we think happened, but not all of the details were available in that sealed file. The Ontario team is heading over to his parents' place today, and Porter is trying to get the full details of the file," Parker explains.

None of the team says anything, but all ten pairs of eyes stare back at her as she puts the pieces together.

"Did he . . . Did he have a history of starting fires or a record of stealing?" She's hesitant to know the answer to her question, but some sick part of her needs to know.

As her gaze locks on each of the ones staring back they're all quick to look away. She thought these guys were supposed to be the toughest. The manliest. But none of them are able to give her a straight answer. Her eyes lock onto Parker's, but he drops his head, running a hand through his hair.

"I think I'm going to be sick." She runs out of the dining room and up the stairs to their bedroom

She barely makes it to the attached bathroom before dry heaves rack her body.

The sound of a door slamming upstairs catapults him into action and he's running after her.

"Dani?"

Anguished cries sound from the middle of the bed where she's sitting with her legs folded up to her chest, her forehead resting on her knees.

He removes his holster and places it on the nightstand before crawling onto the bed and pulling her into his side. "Talk to me."

Her breath hitches when she shakes her head. "I can't believe he's capable of those murders, Parker. Because if he is, that means he was killing while we were together. I lived with a serial killer."

He sighs and wars with himself on whether to tell her the rest of it, but she needs to know.

"Dani, the murders started one and a half years ago. After you had already left."

She lifts her head, and confusion marks her face. "What?"

"He never killed when he was with you."

"What?"

"He never—"

"No, I heard you." She shifts back out of his arms. "He never killed when I was still there," she repeats.

"Danielle."

But she just gets off the bed and starts pacing a hole in the carpet of their bedroom. He moves to sit on the edge of bed with his elbows resting on his knees.

"If I hadn't run from him, those women would still be alive," she whispers.

He opens his arms and she moves to stand between his legs. "You can't think like that, Danielle. He killed before you and he probably would've killed you too if you'd stayed."

"I know. I just can't help but think that maybe those women

would still be alive—"

"Babe, don't do this to yourself. I know it's hard to process right now. And I, for one, am happy that you got out when you did because then I wouldn't have met you and had the opportunity to fall in love with you."

"You love me?" She peers down at him from under her long, black eyelashes.

He places a soft kiss on her lips. "I love you. Funnily enough, Jessica knew before I did."

"I love you too." She grins

Tears are flowing like a river down her face now.

"Oh, baby, I didn't mean to make you cry. I'm sorry."

He spots the Kleenex box still on the bed side table and moves to grab it, but she reaches out and places a hand on his arm. When he turns to face her again she flings herself at him and wraps her arms around his neck, burying her face in his chest.

"I love you," she mumbles in a whisper so small that if he hadn't been paying attention he would've missed it.

He kisses her soft lips. He's fully prepared to end the kiss there, but apparently she has other plans because she's grabbing the hair at the nape of his neck and pressing herself closer to him as she deepens the kiss.

His fingers skim over the smooth skin of her shoulders and down her back to cup her ass. Her legs instantly tighten around his waist when he lifts her and walks them into the bathroom while exploring the delicate flesh of her neck with his tongue.

He kicks the door closed with the heel of his boot, letting her slide down his body until she's standing. He hurriedly turns the shower on before spinning back around to her.

Hooking his thumb under the hem of her black tank top he lets it gently caress her skin while moving it higher, past her belly button, past her breasts, and up until it passes her head and then drops it to the floor. Her black, lacy bra is the next to follow.

He leans down and trails kisses over the tops of her breasts, stopping at her nipple, running his tongue around it, drawing it into a peak, and sucking it into his mouth.

She moans and his cock jumps, straining against his boxers. He moves to her other breast and repeats the same action. Making his way down her stomach, he trails kisses down to the waistband of her black yoga pants.

He runs his fingers under the waistband, sliding it slowly over her hips, and down her thighs, all the while continuing his onslaught of open-mouthed kisses on her skin. Shivers rake her body when he kisses her over her black, lace thong.

He hooks his fingers in her thong and slides it down to join her yoga pants on the floor.

Her eyes are lidded when he lifts her in his arms and carefully stands her up in the shower.

He washes her hair and soaps up her loofa with her cucumber and melon body wash.

She giggles. "I could get to use to this."

He moves her hair off her shoulder placing kisses along the top of her shoulder to her neck. "Hmm, me too, babe."

"Parker! You in here?" Mike yells from the hallway, knocking on the other door to the bathroom.

He groans in frustration at having been interrupted.

She sighs. "Maybe if we ignore them, they'll go away."

"Now there's a thought I could get behind," he says, putting his hands on her hips and pulling her ass closer to his cock.

She laughs. "I bet that's not the only thing you could get behind."

"Dude! Put it back in your pants." Mike pounds on the door again.

"Be there in a sec!" he yells back.

When she turns around to face him, he leans down and crushes his lips to hers, demanding entry. When she complies, their tongues duel for dominance.

Reluctantly he pulls back. "Fuck, I need to go down and talk to the team fast so I can come back up here and finish this."

She grins, and he kisses her lips one more time before regretfully stepping out to get back into his gear. With one last longing look at her gorgeous body, naked in the shower, he turns, leaving the bathroom to make his way downstairs.

Jay glances up from the laptop when he re-enters the dining room. "How'd it go?"

"Better than I thought."

"I bet it did." Mike smirks.

Parker picks up the football from atop the gym bag still sitting on the counter, and throws it at Mike in a perfect spiral. "Fuck off."

"Someone's been practicing their passes." Mike raises an eyebrow.

"My passes are better than yours, asshole," Parker retorts.

"Target was last seen at the flower shop on 48th." Joe hands him the surveillance picture of Adam purchasing a dozen long-stemmed, red roses. "The time stamp was from three days ago."

"Any hits on his credit cards?"

"None so far, sir," Matt says.

"Where do you want to go from here, P?" Jay asks.

"We've already put an alert out at the airport and bus depots, but that won't stop him if he's driving. We put an APB out for his license plate and the make and model of his car," Mike adds.

"From now on we divide the team. We'll partner up so there's at least one of us with Danielle at all times. Joe and I will be with her tonight. Jay and Nick, you two get the next shift. Mike and Cole, you two switch with Jay and Nick in the morning. Clint, you'll take over for Joe tomorrow night. Tyler, Matt, and Caleb, the three of you will be on constant surveillance. If anything new comes in I want to know about it. I don't care what time it is."

"Yes, sir." They all nod in agreement.

Parker's pocket vibrates with an incoming call. It's Kyle. He had Kyle draw a sample of Ashley's blood for the lab to analyze to see if they could identify the drug Adam used.

"Collins," Parker says into the phone.

Jay and Mike aren't paying attention to the rest of the team, instead they're intently watching him pace back and forth between the table and wall separating the kitchen.

"Thanks," he says before hanging up and slipping the phone into his back pocket.

"What was it?" Jay asks.

"Attracurium besilate. It's a paralytic mostly used for anesthesia."

Mike's back straightens with the name of the drug Adam had injected her with. He rummages through the files laying on the table before grabbing the one he was looking for and handing it to Parker.

"You might want to see this."

"Jennifer's file?" Parker looks questionably at Mike.

"Just look at the coroner's report."

"She was injected with the same paralytic."

"Not just injected. The report says she was possibly hooked up to an IV."

"She was still alive when Adam tortured her?" Jay asks, reading over his shoulder.

Mike nods. "She felt everything he did to her."

"Do the other reports say the same thing?" Parker questions Mike.

"We got the coroner's report back from the body found in the parking lot of the visitor's centre. The tox screen came back as the same as Jennifer White's," Nick says, handing Parker the file in front of him.

"'Ashleigh Berg. Twenty-five. Cause of death multiple lacerations to her stomach and chest. Traces of Attracurium besilate still present,'" Parker reads.

"So he tortures them by making them feel every cut, every burn, but they're unable to move the whole time?" Matt asks from the other side of the room.

"Do we have any DNA tying Adam to these murders?" Parker looks up.

"Not yet. He's good at covering his tracks but he's bound to screw up and leave us something," Matt replies.

Parker drops the file on the table, "Keep looking. When we bring that fucker in for questioning I want to be able to charge him with something."

CHAPTER TWENTY-TWO

Oh how he missed this. The game of predator and prey. The pure rush of adrenaline every time they fought for their lives. Every time they ran and he had to drag them back.

Those were the ones he enjoyed best, when they were so determined to fight they actually got a couple hits in. When they managed to leave their mark on him as he did on them. Claw marks down his forearms, a bruise or two. It was a trophy of sorts, and he wore them with pride.

He didn't care much for the ones who just accepted their fate. Those were the ones he killed quickly. But the other ones. The ones who fought. Those were the ones he drew out. The ones he tortured. They begged for their lives every damn time, but he never gave them what they wanted. After all, it was never about them. It was about chasing the rush. It made him feel alive.

He didn't feel much, but when he chased his kill, when he put knife to soft flesh, when the blood flowed, that was when he felt. Those were the only times he felt truly alive.

His latest victim was no exception. She fought beautifully. But in the end her attempts were no match for his pure strength. And when he finally managed to get her strapped down and the IV in her sweet, delicate arm, the pure horror reflected in her eyes at the realization she was quickly losing control of her body was exhilarating.

Cold, emerald eyes stare up at him from the once feisty female lying on the cold, metal surface. His impressive bindings still around her wrists and ankles, the collar still tied around her neck. Her long, dark hair felt like silk sliding through his rough fingers. Her skin was so smooth and soft and untouched. Until the first slide of his blade.

His work of beauty.

He should've been a surgeon. His lines were so clean. So precise. He'd reached perfection. He was finally ready to claim his prize. Ashley, or *Danielle*, or whatever she called herself now.

He takes a deep breath, inhaling the fresh scent of death still lingering in the air around him.

He was ready to drag her back here. To claim her. She thought she could run and hide from him. That her RCMP friends would keep her safe.

Little did she know there was nowhere in this country, no city too big or too small, where he wouldn't or couldn't find her. He'd always find her. For something that magnificent, that beautiful would not go concealed from him.

A slow smirk pulls at his mouth; he would just have to kill the boyfriend first. Men were not his hunt of choice, but he had to get rid of the hindrance. He would just have to make it quick.

A bullet wound or two should do it. If not, then his trusty knife would do the job.

Adam grins. On second thought; knife first, then bullet would be much more rewarding.

Parker and his team tried everything they could to track down Adam's whereabouts, but he seemed to have disappeared off the face of the earth. There'd been no hits on any of his cards or his passport at any airport or border crossing.

Despite knowing Adam is still out there, Ashley's in a surprisingly good mood. Although, she could've done without waking up alone in bed this morning. His hours at the department suck since he made Staff Sergeant, but they've been making it work somehow.

He'd run down the street to Starbucks and brought her back her favourite drink. Kissing her forehead, he'd made sure her alarm was set before leaving for the station.

When her alarm goes off she has just enough time to reheat her salted caramel mocha in the microwave before jumping in her car and getting on the road if she's going to beat the traffic.

On her typical morning commute to the office she always ends up stuck in traffic, without fail. Except for today. It was a smooth drive downtown and she was parked and in the elevator within twenty-five minutes. Which was a huge difference from the typical forty-minute commute.

"Yo, Dani! Sunday night football this week?" Jay calls from the coffee maker behind the reception desk.

Ever since he and the team set up a twenty-four-hour protection detail for her one of the members of the team is always supposed to be with her. Even on the commute into the office but everyone else was called away when another body was found. By the time Jay had called her she was already on her own and just decided to meet him at the office.

She rolls her eyes, stopping at the door to her office. "And hear you brag, for the hundredth time, about your boys being first in their division and the league? No, thanks."

"You just don't want to see us kick your team's ass."

"That too," she throws back before shutting her office door and walking around her desk to wake up the computer and go through the countless emails and requests she knows are waiting for her.

While she's sipping her coffee and waiting for her computer to boot up her eyes land on a single, long-stemmed, red rose sitting on her desk, and her blood runs cold.

There's only one person she knows who would leave a single, red rose for her to find.

Under the rose is a small typed note.

I told you I would kill him.

"Jay!"

CHAPTER TWENTY-THREE

Why can't he ever find his keys when he's in a hurry?

He decided to come home before the next briefing but forgot Danielle was in the office today. Usually he just throws his keys down anywhere, then she finds them, and gets frustrated at him for never putting them on the entry table.

Eventually, she ends up putting them there herself. But she's not here, which means he has no fucking clue where his keys are.

He's bent over the couch lifting seat cushions when a sharp pain penetrates his side. He looks down in time to see a knife, covered in his blood, being pulled from his body.

"Parker, I presume."

His eyes follow the knife, past the hand holding it, and all the way up the arm and shoulder to his face until they land on eyes as black as midnight.

Adam.

His hands immediately fly to the open wound that's dripping with fresh blood. As far as wounds go it's a clean cut but it still hurts like a bitch.

"You know you're taller than what I expected," Adam continues.

Parker's training takes over and he lands a solid right hook to Adam's jaw.

Adam stumbles back, dropping the knife, and Parker takes the opportunity to land another right hook to Adam's face then an uppercut to his stomach. But Adam starts laughing hysterically when he straightens back up, pulling a 9mm from the waistband of his jeans.

The shooting pain from his side is a killer, but he's trying to rely on his training and ignore the pain until he's taken out Adam. This guy has been a ghost for six months and then suddenly shows up at their house with a knife and a gun.

"Well, don't you play dirty?" Adam sneers.

"You're the one who brought a knife to a fist fight. What? Didn't think you were man enough to fight me without the weapons?" Parker knows he's getting him riled up but he can't help it. It's been months since he's wanted to get this guy in his line of sight, and show him what a real man looks like, for beating Ashley all those years ago. "Oh, yeah, I forgot. You're not a man at all.

You're a coward who hits women and then stalks them for years."

Adam snickers. "She liked it when I hit her. She got off on it. And when I would throw her down and bind her hands she'd resist and say no at first, but I could tell, secretly, she wanted it."

"You're a sick son of a bitch."

Adam sneers. "Maybe, but I'll be the one walking away alive and after I've killed you I'm going after her. She'll be mine again. And you . . . well, you'll be dead."

Adam levels his gun at Parker and pulls the trigger, the bullet connecting with his shoulder with enough force to cause him to fall back.

Adam lands a kick to his ribs forcing him to roll onto his back. Blackness starts clouding his vision and shivers rake his body. He can't ignore the pain any longer. Adam was right, he wasn't able to keep his promise to her.

Adam leans in to whisper in his ear, "You lose, Parker. She's mine."

As if she heard his last thought she appears like an angel in his vision. Long, dark hair flowing over her shoulder. She's calling his name but he can't respond to her. Then his whole world goes black.

CHAPTER TWENTY-FOUR

She feels like she got run over by a semitruck. Her body aches in places she never knew could hurt this much. Her head is pounding and she feels like she's going to get sick at any minute.

The memory of what happened earlier starts to play behind her eyelids like a scene in a horror movie. The note under the rose. Yelling for Jay. Frantically calling Parker's cell phone with no answer. Jay told her to wait and that he was getting his team together, but she couldn't wait. So while he had his back turned she snuck out of the office and raced home.

Running through the front door to see him lying in a puddle of blood. His blood. She's frantically looking around for her cell phone but she couldn't dial 9-1-1 because the room spun and went black.

Parker.

He wasn't breathing and there was so much blood.

A sob leaves her throat at the thought of him lying dead in their house. Oh, God. She refuses to believe that he's actually dead. He can't be dead.

The sound of a floorboard creaking makes her eyes snap open and scan the room. She has no idea where she is and it's too dark to see anything. Every time she tries to move her arms and legs they get snapped back to the position they were previously in.

Both her wrists and ankles are bound. Tightly. She tries yanking on the bindings, but they don't budge. Instead, she can feel the rope cutting into her skin every time she moves. The knots tighten with every pull.

Her heart races, and her breathing picks up as she tries, unsuccessfully, to pull again and again at the bindings holding her down. Her wrists and ankles are throbbing with pain, but she doesn't care. She needs to get at least one wrist free. Her body visibly shakes with adrenaline when try after try fails.

Where the fuck is she?

"You can struggle to your heart's content but you're not going to loosen my bindings, *Danielle*."

That voice.

Adam.

Her head snaps to the side. It's too dark to see into the corner, but she knows he's there. She can feel his eyes on her now. The bastard is smiling too; he always did enjoy watching people struggle. Financially, emotionally, physically. He enjoyed it all.

"Where am I, Adam?"

"You can scream all you want. There's no one around for miles."

"Why are you doing this?" She trembles.

"Because I can, Ashley. Because nobody will stop me."

"So you kidnapped me because you can?"

"I told you I'd have you again, Ashley."

"You're delusional and a sick fuck." She's still trying to twist and turn her wrists in hopes that at least one of the knots will relax. She just needs it to loosen about an inch and then maybe she can wiggle her hand out.

"Possibly, but I was right. I do have you again."

"You killed him."

"It was . . . ." Adam inhales deeply before continuing his recount, "exhilarating watching his life slip away, knowing I caused it to happen."

Her eyes burn with unshed tears, and a piercing scream leaves her throat. She shuts her eyes as tears stream down her cheeks. Adam killed him, and for what? Because she was selfish. She didn't want to let him go. She didn't want to lose him but she ended up losing him anyway. Adam was true to his word.

"No, don't shut your eyes. Look at me!" Adam moves away from where he was seated in the darkened corner. The bed dips when he sits and grabs a hold of her face with one of his hands, squishing her cheeks together. "Look at me, Ashley! I want to see those pretty, green eyes when I tell you how much he fought for his life. How much he fought for you. He put up quite a good fight too. Bastard even got in a good hit or two, but I was stronger. Oh, Ashley! You should've seen it," Adam recounts enthusiastically.

"No!" she shrieks, turning her head, yanking her face out of his grasp.

"That rush of adrenaline after the first shot, the first stab, the first spill of blood. There's nothing else like it." Adam's fingers move to her stomach and run up her torso under her shirt. "And the blood . . . it was so warm leaving his body. It's amazing how as the blood was leaving his body I was watching the life leave his eyes." Adam's hand finds her breast as his finger starts circling her nipple over her bra.

Nausea threatens its way up from her stomach. Adam just murdered the man she loves with all her heart, and now those same hands are touching her while he recounts everything he did to Parker. Adam doesn't even show an ounce of remorse for what he did.

"You feel so good, Ashley. I can't wait to taste you again. It's been too fucking long."

She pulls frantically at the bindings holding her in place and thrashes from side to side in a wasted effort to get away from him. "No!"

He leans in close to her ear, she can feel his breath on her cheek. "Remember what happened the last time you said no to me, Ashley. Nobody says no to me. Nobody."

Adam is in a frenzy now, ripping her shirt from her body and yanking her jeans down to her ankles. Somewhere in the distance she hears the button from her Levi's hit the wood floor.

"Adam, please! Please don't!" she begs, but he doesn't hear her.

His eyes darken and a smirk pulls at his mouth.

She's trying to kick out and thrust her knees up from under him in hopes that something connects, but it doesn't. Adam has given her bindings very little give, making any movement useless and extremely painful.

From somewhere in the rest of the house comes the first five seconds of *Click Click Boom* from Saliva. His ringtone. She remembers that it used to be his favourite song years ago. So much so that when he got his new phone Adam just had to have it as his ringtone.

"Fuck!" Adam yells getting off the bed and slamming the door behind him.

Tears are still streaming down her face, coming so fast that they're clouding her vision. She's grateful to whomever is on the other side of that phone call and she's hoping that they keep Adam on the phone long enough for her to figure out a way to get of here. Better yet, she hopes that he gets called away from wherever this   is

CHAPTER TWENTY-FIVE

"How is he?"

Voices float in from somewhere in the darkness. A constant beep of a machine sounds from next to him. He tries to pry his eyes open, but they feel so heavy.

"Multiple wounds . . . barely beating . . . lucky to be alive . . . missed . . . his artery . . . able to stop internal bleed . . ."

She's mine.

He's not sure how long he's been out, but every inch of his body fucking hurts, and he has a bad case of dry mouth. He tries opening his mouth to speak, but all that comes out is a low groan.

"Parker?" Kat is sitting next to his hospital bed with a magazine laying open on her legs. Jay, Alice, and Mike are walking back into the room when his eyes finally focus.

"Need. Water." He struggles to get the words out, past his dry throat. His voice sounds rough and not at all like his.

"I'll call Dr. Reynolds," Alice says before leaving.

"How are you feeling?" Jay asks, now standing behind Kat's chair.

Before he can think of a reply Mike chimes in, "Dude, what the fuck?"

Kat looks at Mike, annoyed, before turning back to Parker. "I believe what Mike meant was what happened? Where's Dani?"

Danielle!

She's mine.

He tries reaching over to the bed side table where he hopes his phone is located, but the damn IV they have him connected to keeps pulling, preventing him from getting hold of his cell.

"Phone."

Kat gives him a skeptical look before reaching over to grab his phone, handing it to him. Not even five seconds later he's holding the ringing phone to his ear, praying that she decided to go straight to Anne's after work instead of stopping by the house first.

"Hi, you've reached Danielle. Sorry I couldn't come to the phone but if you leave a message—"

Voicemail

Fuck! He hits redial and tries again, but her voicemail comes on every time. Son of a bitch! He hits redial again but he knows in his gut that Adam already has her. He told Parker himself he was going to take her, right before Parker passed out from the pain.

His head is no longer foggy, he's wide awake and alert now. He promised he would always protect her and right now he's failing. But if he's going to do this and live to tell about it then he's going to need some major help.

"She's not going to answer," Jay eventually says, defeated.

"What do you mean she's not going to answer? You were supposed to be watching her, Jay," Parker accuses.

"I was at the office with her when she got Adam's note. I told her to wait till I got a hold of the team before we met them at the house but when I turned around she was gone." Jay hangs his head.

"Parker, if Adam has Dani— "

"If he hurts her, Nicole, he won't live to see another day," Parker reassures her.

"Fuck," Mike says under his breath.

His thoughts exactly.

"Parker, it's been a day. What if he . . ." Kat can't bring herself to finish her sentence.

Twenty-four hours is a long time to hold someone against their will without killing them. But he knows Adam doesn't want to kill her. He's sick and delusional but he loves her. He wouldn't kill her unless he thought there was no way he could have her to himself. Jay walks out into the hallway when his phone rings.

Adam wouldn't kill her because he thinks he succeeded in killing him. "Don't say it, Nic. She's not dead. She can't be."

"Parker—" Mike starts, moving closer.

"No." He throws off the hospital blankets and removes the stupid IV line before pushing himself up off the bed.

"Parker! What are you doing?" Alice exclaims when she walks back into his room with Dr. Reynolds in tow.

"I'm not going to lie helpless while that sick fuck has my girl."

Mike and Dr. Reynolds converge in front of him, blocking his path to the closet and his clothes.

"You need to take it easy still, Collins. You lost a lot of blood, and your stitches are still fresh." Reynolds has his hands up to stop him, but he continues his advance.

"You won't be helping her if you walk out of here early and end up back here with an infection or worse," Mike adds.

Fuck that, this is what they're trained for. It has now become a hostage situation. He'll deal with the stitches and any other injury as they need attention but he's not staying in the damn hospital. "I don't care. I need to find her. We're trained for this."

"I get it, but all of our teams have been working round the clock to track down his whereabouts."

Before Mike can continue to convince him to stay put, Jay walks back through the door, pocketing his phone. "Got a last location. The fucker hides his tracks well but he slipped up this time."

"Dude, what the fuck?" Mike, always the one with the exceptional vocabulary.

Jay shrugs. "He needs to find his girl. You know that as well as I do trying to stop him right now would be about the same as banging your head repeatedly against a brick wall and expecting the wall to move. We might as well help him and make sure his ass doesn't die this time."

Mike sighs, looking from Parker to Jay and back again. "Fine, but I'm coming with you." Mike turns back and points his finger at Parker. "And we're calling for reinforcements."

Dr. Reynolds clears his throat. "You know, as your doctor and family friend, I'm going to officially have to advise against you leaving."

"And unofficially?" Parker asks

"Unofficially, go get your girl. Just try not to get stabbed this time or worse. Don't come back dead."

"No promises, Doc."

"Right," he mumbles under his breath while walking away to complete his rounds. As soon as Dr. Reynolds is out of earshot he turns back to Jay.

"I'm going to need a gun."

"I have a .45 in my glove compartment."

He nods. "That'll do."

"So, what? You're going to go all *Expendables* in bloody clothes with one gun and one round?" Alice chimes in with a raised eyebrow.

"Why not? Statham and Stallone did it," Mike retorts.

"Ah, no they didn't. They had a lot more fire power and a whole team. Plus, that was a movie. I thought guys were knowledgeable about this stuff," Alice fires back with her hands on her hips.

He can sense that Mike is gearing up for an argument, but they don't have time for this shit. They need to get out there and find her. "Look, you guys can argue action movies another day, but we need to move."

"Jessica and I will go back to our apartment," Kat says, walking up to Jay and placing her hand on his arm. "Please call us when you find her." Her eyes plead with him before she and Alice turn and continue their way down to the elevators.

"The guys have the surveillance video from the gas station Adam was last seen at. They're waiting for us to get to my house before they watch it." Jay looks up from his phone and to Parker expectantly.

"Jessica's right. We'll stop at my place to grab clean clothes and my Glock."

"You really want to go back there, P?" Mike looks hesitant.

"It might actually help if he can find anything out of place that we might have missed," Jay counters.

"You think he grabbed her from the house?" Parker asks.

"That's what we're thinking. Her fingerprints were found close to where we found you."

"She lives there, obviously her fingerprint would be in the house."

"Parker, she had your blood on her hand when she made the print."

"She found me?"

Jay nods. "She did, and it looks like she was about to call 9-1-1 before she was taken. Her cell phone was lying next to your head, but she never got the chance it hit dial."

"So, Adam probably thinks I'm dead."

"It's a possibility. When Mike and I found you we had a hard time finding a pulse. Your heartbeat had slowed drastically, and you'd lost a lot of blood."

"I hate to even ask this, but would Adam kill her?" Mike questions

Remembering his thoughts from earlier he shakes his head, "He's sick and delusional but he loves her. He wouldn't kill her unless he thought there was no way he could have her. If he thinks he succeeded in getting rid of me then he has no reason to kill her."

"Okay. Would she provoke him if she thought you were dead?"

"Dude, that's some Shakespearian shit." Both Jay and Parker

looked over to Mike with brows drawn together.

"What? I know Romeo and Juliet." Mike shrugs.

"No, I don't think she would. She's scared, but if I know her, she'll be trying to keep her cool and look for a way out of wherever he has her."

"Let's get the team over to your house. We'll set up home base there," Jay suggests.

The three of them leave the hospital to meet up with the rest of the team at Parker's house. As soon as they're through the front door they do a sweep of the house. When nothing comes up Parker races upstairs to shower, change into his spare tactical gear, and grab his extra firearm.

When he finally makes it downstairs Jay has already briefed the three teams on the information they have and watched the surveillance video from the gas station.

"What do we have?" Parker asks, strapping on his vest.

"Matt and Joe just talked to the gas station attendant. He said he recognized Adam from the picture they showed him. Apparently, Adam has gone in there regularly to fill up his car or purchase other stuff," Jay says, pointing to the attendant on the laptop screen.

"Does he know where Adam's staying?"

"He does. He told the guys that the entire area is taken up by farmland. There are only three houses within fifteen kilometres. He and his wife live in one and he says he knows the couple who live on the land attached to his. But the owner of the land on the opposite side had a family emergency out west so he decided to rent it out. The attendant doesn't know who the guy rented it to, but he's only ever seen Adam come and go."

"Do we have an address?"

"Matt should be sending it through now."

"Let's gear up."

"Heat sensor is showing only one person inside," Matt says, running up to meet them as the team exits both SUVs.

"Do you have a layout of the house yet?" Parker asks, scanning the exterior of the house and surrounding farm land.

It smells like old horse shit out here, like someone just

abandoned their horses and has been gone for some time.

"Three bedrooms. One on the far right side, the other two on the far left side. Separated by a living room and kitchen. Bathroom is on the right, next to the bedroom," Joe says, joining them.

"Danielle?"

"She's in the room on the right, sir." Joe points to the side of the house directly in front of him.

"Can you get a visual?" Mike asks.

"Working on it, sir."

"All right, let's go over our entry one more time." Jay moves toward the second SUV parked behind them and lays out a floor plan of the farm house on the hood.

"Mike, you and your team take the back entrance. Parker and I will take the front with Nick, Joe, and Clint. If the target shows up, shoot on sight."

The teams nod their understanding before dispersing to check their weapons and ammunition and separating into their respective teams.

"You okay, man?" Jay slaps Parker on the back, and he winces. "Shit, sorry."

"I'll be fine once I know she's safe."

"Dude, you sure you want to go in there? Matt can go in your place," Mike says, coming up on his other side.

He nods. "I need to know that after today he won't be able to hurt another hair on her head. That she'll finally be free and able to start fully healing from the years of unseen torture and sick games. I need to know that even after being injured I can still protect her, that guys like Adam will never win. But I swear to all that is holy, if he hurts one hair on her head I will hunt him down and I will kill him. No one threatens my woman."

Mike sighs and places his hand on Parker's other shoulder. "Let's go get your girl."

"Sound off when ready," Jay says into his mic.

"Ready." Mike replies.

"Okay, let's do this fast so that we can get the hell out of here. On three." Jay raises his arm and counts on his fingers: One. Two. Three.

Parker doesn't hear or see anything else after the initial knocking down of both doors. His heart is hammering in his chest and all he can think of is that she is somewhere in this house, and the only thing stopping him from getting to her are four walls

"Clear!"

"Clear!"

"Staff Sergeant!" Clint yells from across the house.

Parker runs towards him and stops dead in his tracks when he enters the room Clint's standing outside of.

She's blindfolded and chained to a queen-sized bed. Her shirt lies in tatters on the floor, and her jeans are pooled around her ankles. Her underwear and bra are still intact. Bruises adorn her arms, neck, and jaw, and her lip is split. Her face is streaked with dried tears and black mascara.

"Danielle."

Her head turns to the direction of his voice. "Parker?"

He doesn't waste any time untying the blindfold and cutting through the ropes around her wrists and ankles. The sight of the bruising around them almost bringing him to his knees. "Oh, baby." Ignoring the pain in his chest, he gathers her up in his arms and swears to himself that he'll never let her go.

She grips the back of his shirt while she buries her nose in his neck and cries harder.

"You're not dead," she says when her tears have slowed down enough.

"It takes a lot more than that to kill me."

"You came for me?" she asks, disbelief present in her eyes.

He knows there's more meaning behind that question than just him tracking her down after Adam took her. All her life she was used to people not choosing her. She was made to feel like she wasn't worth the effort, that she wasn't good enough. But he will always put her first. And he will make sure he spends the rest of his life proving to her that she's worth the effort. "Baby, I'll always come for you. I don't care how hard you fight me, Danielle. You can push me away again and again, but I'll keep coming back. I'll keep fighting for you. For us. Because you're worth it, Danielle. Nothing and no one will keep me from you."

Fresh tears fall down her cheeks as she flings herself at him again, wrapping her arms around his neck.

He winces when her body hits his.

"Fuck, I'm sorry." She pulls back looking at his chest.

"It's okay, but we might need to take a trip back to the hospital. I think I may have started bleeding again."

"Parker, you didn't have to—"

"Don't finish that sentence. Yes, I did. I made you a promise that I'd protect you and I intend to keep that promise, Danielle." His thumb gently slides back and forth over her cheek, "I love you."

"I love you too."

"Sorry to interrupt, but you might want to see this, P." Mike knocks on the open door and inclines his head for him to follow.

Mike leads him into the bedroom on the other side of the house where Jay is standing over a wooden chest that looks like it had been dragged out of the closet.

"What did you find?" he inquires, walking over to Jay and the chest.

"Not exactly sure."

"Trophies?" Mike suggests.

"It's possible. There's everything in here from jewelry, and driver's licenses, to women's underwear." Jay hands him the driver's license he's holding.

"Jennifer White," Parker reads.

"Isn't that the name of the wife?" Mike asks

"It was the name of his wife," Jay corrects.

"Still can't believe he'd kill his own wife," Mike states.

"It makes sense," Parker reasoned. "He didn't have any use for her anymore when he became partner in her father's law firm. She was just a means to an end."

"'Till death do they part,' I guess," Mike says.

"Clint, get this all bagged for evidence and to the lab. If there are other victim's out there we need to identify them and figure out where he buried the bodies," Jay orders.

"Yes, sir,"

"If he buried them," Parker adds.

"If?" Mike questions.

"Some serial killers don't bury the bodies of their victim's. Ed Gein wore the skin of his."

"*Silence of the Lambs*," Jay comments.

"He was a psychopath though," Mike says.

"Adam fits the profile," Jay concludes.

"He tortured and killed animals as a kid. His parents said he tried starting fires before that. And he killed his three-year-old sister without remorse. In fact, even at a young age he was able to fake his grief over her death so nobody would suspect him. He's charming, he works his way up to partner in his law firm in under two years. That's practically unheard of. Who knows how many others he's killed over the years," Parker offers.

"Shit," Mike says.

"'Not all criminals are psychopaths and not all psychopaths are criminals.' Dr. George Simon said that," Parker says.

"But in this case he was both," Jay comments.

Not long after getting her to the hospital to get checked out, Parker receives a call from Constable Smith. After further investigation into her dad's death the OPP have ruled his death a homicide. Parker lets him know about Adam and what Ashley had told him about Adam's last encounter with her father, as well as his suspicion that Adam might have had more to do with her father's death. Constable Smith agrees to get his team to look into it more from his side.

CHAPTER TWENTY-SIX

"Hey, princess!" Parker greets, opening the door for Anne and Bella

"I brought *Zootopia!*" Bella exclaims, running past him into the living room.

"How is she?" Anne asks, stepping through the front door as he props it open.

He shrugs. "She's stubborn. She says she's okay but she's having a hard time with everything."

Anne nods. "Do you think it'd be okay if I went up to talk to her?"

"You go ahead. Bell and I will be down here watching her movie."

Anne stands hesitantly at the open door to Parker and Ashley's bedroom with one hand poised to knock.

"Hey, Anne. Come in," Ashley says, noticing her as she walks out of their bathroom.

"Hey, Dani. How are you doing?"

"Okay. I've had better days but I'm okay."

"Good. I'm glad you're safe."

"What's wrong, Anne?"

"Nothing."

"Anne," she challenges.

"It really is nothing. You've already been through so much, this doesn't seem as important anymore."

"Come on, Anne. Tell me. I could use something to distract myself with anyways."

Anne raises an eyebrow questioningly. "I thought you said you were okay."

"I am," she protests, staring unflinchingly back at Anne.

Anne sighs. "Okay, fine. Carl, my ex-husband, called me the other night."

"What did he want?"

"He apologized for the way he left things and wanted to know if I'd be up for going for coffee and maybe revisit giving him another chance."

"And how do you feel about that? Do you want to?"

"I never stopped loving him, Dani. I wasn't the one who wanted the divorce. But he walked out at a time when I needed him the most. How do I know that when things get hard again, he won't do the same?"

"You don't."

"That's not helping." Anne frowns.

"I know, but it's the truth. You don't know if he'll walk out again but you have to do what you feel is the right thing to do. If you still love him, and he still loves you, then why not go for a coffee and see how things go." Ashley smiles reassuringly. "I'm not saying you have to remarry the guy, but go and see what he has to say then take it one day at a time from there."

"Thanks, Dani."

"No problem. I consider you a good friend, Anne. And I hope you know that if you ever need to talk I'll be here."

"That goes both ways." Anne levels a challenging look at Ashley.

"Fair enough. I'm not okay. Ever since Parker and the team found me and brought me home I've been having nightmares. I wake up out of a deep sleep, sitting bolt upright and in a cold sweat."

"Does he know?"

"I'm sure he does, but I don't want to burden him even more with my nightmares. And he hasn't said anything." Ashley glances up from under long, black eyelashes with sadness in her eyes. "Is it bad that I wish the team would just find him and kill him? Then maybe my nightmares would go away, and the families of all those women would be able to sleep better at night knowing the bastard who killed their daughters will never be coming back."

"I think that's a normal, human reaction. This guy lured you in years ago with his charm and was able to, essentially, hold you hostage, maybe not physically but mentally. And when you thought you were finally free of him, he came back and not only did he attempt to kill you and Parker but he killed your father. So no, I don't think it's bad."

Ashley wraps her arms around Anne and brings her in for a hug. "Thanks, Anne."

"Do the guys have a plan now?"

"Parker is putting me back under twenty-four/seven protection until Adam is taken out or brought into custody. Apparently, I wasn't the only one with a new identity. That's why they didn't get any hits on his credit cards. He had other cards issued under a different name."

"Speaking of identity. Will you be going back to Ashley after he's caught?"

Danielle shakes her head. "Ashley was a weak, scared girl from my past. I don't even know who she is anymore. She's definitely not the person I've become since moving here and she's not the person I want to be again. Danielle is my future."

Anne pulls Danielle in for another hug. "I agree."

"Thanks for coming by, Anne. I think I really needed another female to talk to and I didn't want to bother Nic and Jessica with Adam stuff anymore than I have."

"It's no problem. Like I said, it goes both ways. Bella is downstairs watching *Zootopia* with Parker." Anne laughs. "I need to get to work though, I'm already running a bit late. Thanks for the advice on Carl."

"Anytime," Danielle says, walking Anne to the hallway.

Parker refused to go back to the hospital to get his gunshot and stab wounds checked out. He did, after a lot of arguing with Danielle and convincing on Porter's part; however, agree to a two week paid leave, effective immediately. Bella may have also helped to convince him.

He would do anything for that little girl, but Danielle also thinks he secretly enjoyed having her stay over every day for the last week to play video games with him. The two of them have spent hours on the couch playing *Minecraft*.

On numerous occasions she's heard Bella try to convince him to let her play *Call of Duty* and *Assassin's Creed*. He can never say no to her so instead he ruffled her hair and then distracted her with the Lego Batman game and new toys he'd bought.

Most times it works to distract her from her original argument, but those times are becoming fewer and farther between. She's almost six, and Danielle's fairly certain that when it comes to him, she'll always get her way.

The thought of Bella's birthday is what makes her finally take her eyes off of the two of them in the living room and focus on the to-do list in front of her. Her sixth birthday is next week and Anne asked her to plan it for her.

Actually her exact words were, "Please, Danielle. I suck big, hairy monkey balls at party planning, and with everything that's happened the last several years, Bella deserves at least one nice birthday party."

Needless to say, she agreed. Now she's sitting at their kitchen counter with a blank notepad in front of her, the Pinterest app on her phone open with "party ideas for a six-year-old girl" typed into the search bar.

The first thing that pops up is a pony party, but she immediately scrolls past it. That's not Bella at all. The next one under that is a Dory themed fruit punch, and that's when the idea hits her. Bella liked the indoor pool at his old house but she loves the one that they have in this new house.

After what had happened with Adam, Dani and Parker agreed they'd never be able to move on from the memories if they had to live in the same house they were both attacked in. So they sold that house and ended up finding one they loved even more about a block away.

The new one also had an indoor pool, at Bella's request, but it also had tons of backyard space so she could run around to her heart's content whenever she came over.

That kid would move in and spend all of her time downstairs in the pool if they let her. But that would make for the perfect party.

Excitedly, she shuts down the app and immediately sends Anne a message with her idea and waits for a reply.

Anne: You're a genius! We'll go shopping for supplies this weekend.

Danielle: Sounds good.

"You look happy," Parker says, kissing her temple before going to grab a drink out of the fridge.

"Finally figured out what to do for Bella's birthday party next week."

"Oh, yeah?"

She nods, grinning at him when he sits down on the bar stool beside her. He's still moving slowly today, but the doctors say he's recovering fairly quickly. Faster than what they expected.

"Care to share?"

"What? With you? Mr. 'I can't keep anything a secret from Bella'?"

He tips his head back, laughing. "Okay, you're right. I can never keep anything from her."

She goes back to jotting down her ideas on the notepad, expecting him to go back to playing *Minecraft* with Bella, but he doesn't move.

"How are you doing, Danielle?" Concern laces his voice and she almost wishes he would've gone back to the living room. She knows she can't keep avoiding the question every time someone asks her.

She shrugs, turning to face him. "I thought I would've been okay, but part of me still expects him to pop up somewhere I least expect. I spent years thinking I was free of him and of my past, but then he found me and has spent the last year tormenting me. I was some kind of twisted prize to him, and when he couldn't have me he killed people. He even tried to kill you . . . he almost succeeded in killing you." She shakes her head, trying to dislodge the memories of the last couple of months. "At least the nightmares are getting less and less."

"It's only been a month. Don't be surprised if some of them come back later."

"I know." She glances up at him. "I made an appointment with Dr. Stevenson."

"The counsellor?"

"For years I tried to do everything by myself, and look where that got me. I think I'd like to try doing it differently this time. I just feel that in some way I'm partly responsible for him killing all those women."

"Danielle, you're in no way responsible for what Adam chose to do, and you're not alone this time. You have the girls and you have me. I'll be right there with you every step of the way."

"How did I get so lucky?" She smiles

He shakes his head. "I'm the lucky one."

"Parker! I need help!" Bella hollers from the living room.

He grins and stands up. "I'm proud of you, babe." He kisses her forehead before heading back to help Bella with her game.

❖

Bella's birthday goes off without a hitch, and there are about fifteen five- and six-year-olds taking over the pool room.

She's setting the last of the snacks on the food table when Anne bounces up to her. "Danielle! This is amazing. Thank you so much for doing it." She throws her arms around her in a bear hug.

Laughing, she hugs her back. "It was no problem, Anne. It was actually kind of fun."

Anne's expression turns serious, and her smiles fades when her eyes find Bella splashing around in the pool with her classmates. "If anything happens to me promise me you and Parker will look after Bella," she whispers.

"Anne—"

"Promise me, Danielle. Please."

Unease fills Danielle and she wonders if there's something that Anne hasn't told Parker or the team.

Anne turns to face her, her eyes sad and brimming with tears. "Please, Danielle."

"I promise. But, Anne, if something's going on you should let Parker or Jay know."

Anne shakes her head, "Nothing's going on. I've just never been on a plane before. It'll be my first time being on one when Carl and I leave tomorrow for our get reacquainted trip."

Danielle wraps her up in another hug while tears stream down her face. "Oh, Anne, flying can actually be kind of fun." She inclines her head to where Bella is doing the doggie paddle with her arms in floaties.

"Bella will always have the three of us looking over her. Parker already thinks of her as his own. And, well, you've seen how protective Bella is over him too." They both giggle at the memory of Bella giving women her version of the stink eye whenever she caught them looking at him while they were grocery shopping.

"Thank you," Anne whispers before removing herself from Danielle's arms and going in search of the birthday girl.

CHAPTER TWENTY-SEVEN

"Collins," Parker answers his ringing phone.

"Sergeant, we have a location on White," Cole says from the other side.

"Text me the address and get the rest of the team to meet us there," he barks into his phone before hitting end.

This was going to end tonight. After he and his team take out Adam, Danielle can finally start the healing process.

That wannabe soldier thought he could beat Adam. Why couldn't he just have stayed dead, then Adam wouldn't have needed to go and do what he did.

He didn't care though; he would've hunt his current prey regardless. The bitch didn't know when to just go away.

Every time he got close to Ashley, she would fucking be there. Her and those other two bitches Ashley hangs around. That's okay though, because he plans on getting rid of them too.

Adam was just glad she didn't have her bratty, fucking kid with her. He'd spotted her struggling to get a suitcase in her car. It was the perfect opportunity if he ever saw one.

He wasn't disappointed either, she'd fought the most out of all his previous victims. He'd almost regretted having to kill her. Almost.

He'd just poured himself a couple fingers of whiskey when the door to his upscale condo gets blown open and men in tactical gear rush in.

When they turn to enter the living room, Adam aims and fires off as many rounds as he can, forcing them back to take cover behind the wall separating the entry from the living room. But he doesn't move from his spot, standing in front of the couch.

Bullets fly back and forth between their team and Adam. When Adam's handgun runs out of bullets, Parker takes full advantage and fires off one more round. Hitting right him between the eyes.

"Target eliminated. Search the rooms!" Parker says into his mic.

A hush falls over the station the moment Parker walks through the double glass doors. Everyone has stopped what they're doing, and all eyes are on him.

"What's going on?" He looks at Jay

"Another body was found. Young female, early twenties."

"Where? Was she one of Adam's victims?"

"Her body was stuffed into the trunk of his car, but Parker—"

Mike walks up next to Jay and lays a hand on Parker's shoulder.

"It's Anne," Mike says solemnly.

Dread sits like cement in his gut. Danielle has been trying to get ahold of Anne for the last few days, but Anne's phone has been sending every call to voicemail without ringing. They just assumed Anne and her ex-husband were still working things through, and she'd call once they got back to their hotel.

"Can I see the file?"

Jay shakes his head. "You don't have to see that, man. It's not pretty. Don't do that to yourself."

When he doesn't seem like he's going to be convinced, Jay reluctantly hands him the file.

His gut clenches as Anne's name stares up at him from the first page.

Name: Anne Graham
Born: January 26, 1989.
Deceased: September 30, 2016.
Age: 27
Parents: deceased.
No emergency contact listed.
Younger sister: Gabriella Graham.
Born: June 18, 2010.
Age: 6.

She was killed yesterday before they raided his condo. That's why she was still in his trunk, he hadn't had time to bury her body yet. When he flips the page up nausea rolls through him as his eyes take in the pictures of the crime scene.

Anne's naked body is laying bent in half in the trunk. Her lifeless eyes staring up at the camera. Ligature marks on her wrists and ankles. Identical marks to the rope burns on Danielle's wrists and ankles. Cigarette burns decorate her arms and thighs. A clean line is visible running across her neck.

"He tortured her." Parker's voice is barely above a whisper.

"Looks like that was his plan." Mike pries the file out of his limp hands.

"Something must have spooked him to make him slit her throat," Jay adds.

"What happens to Bell now?"

"Porter is trying to get ahold of the ministry now. They'll probably be taking her until something else can be arranged." Jay slaps him on the shoulder. "Look, man, there's nothing for you to do here. Why don't you go home and we'll bring over some beers later?"

He spots the inspector at the elevator bank and rushes towards him.

"Hey, Inspector, heard you were calling the ministry about the latest victim's sister."

Victim. Parker hates referring to Anne as that. She was never a victim until Adam made her one. Anne was a fighter just like Bella will be.

"Just about to head to my office to make the call."

"I'd like to be there when you do and I'd like to be the one to tell Bella."

"Bella?"

"Gabriella . . ."

"Ah, the younger sister. Didn't know you knew the victim and her sister."

"Yes, sir."

"It's heartbreaking that little girl is going to end up in the system anyway."

"Actually, sir. That's what I'd like to talk to the ministry about. Bella already knows me. Hell, I consider her and Anne family. I have the resources. . ."

"What are you saying, son?"

"I'm saying I'd like to adopt her."

"You want to take on a six-year-old?"

"Yes, sir."

"Have you talked to Danielle about this?"

"No, sir. But I know she'll agree with me when I tell her about Anne."

Porter sighs weighing his options. "All right. It's not my call on the adoption, but you can be there when I call them and see what they say. No guarantees though, Parker. They may still take her for a day or two."

"I realize that, Mitch. But I need to try. I wouldn't be able to forgive myself if I let her get lost in the foster care system."

The inspector pats him on the back as they step out of the elevator and onto the floor heading towards his office. "Okay, let's go make the call."

There's a war of emotions going on inside him as he drives home. The ministry has agreed to look over his request to adopt Bella, and in the meantime she'll still get to stay with him and Danielle. They said it was better she be with someone she knows while she's grieving the loss of her sister.

Bella still doesn't know about Anne or that Anne never did make it to the airport with Carl. That tidbit of information was delegated solely for him to tell her.

He's dreading having to look that little girl in the eyes and tell her another one of her family members has passed away. Bella didn't need to know the details. No six-year-old should know that their sister was brutally murdered at the hands of a psychopathic serial killer.

Pulling into his driveway he throws the car into park, and his fists pound the steering wheel in anger. Anger about what happened to Anne, and what Bella will have to go through now. Anger at what Dani experienced. Anger at the knowledge that Anne had died in a similar fashion to what he had found Danielle in in Adam's farm house.

Years of anger and frustration, over his family and the pain that Danielle had endured, was taken out on the steering wheel, and it felt fucking good to finally let it all out.

Maybe he should start sparing with Mike at the new MMA Gym.

He'd already called Dani from the hospital and filled her in on what happened. After he told her what he'd told Porter about adopting Bella, she wholeheartedly agreed that it was the right thing to do and that they wouldn't tell Bella how Anne died until she asked and she was much older.

She said she'd go and pick up Bella from school, and they'd meet him back at the house.

The smell of freshly baked, chocolate chip cookies invades his nose as soon as he steps through the front door and drops his wallet and keys on the entryway table. Danielle likes to bake whenever she's nervous or anxious.

His two girls are cuddled on the couch under a huge, fleece blanket, despite the melting temperature outside. *The Good Dinosaur* is playing on the TV.

"Can never go wrong with dinosaurs."

Bella pops her head up at the sound of his voice, and, like always, he crouches down and opens his arms so she can run straight into them.

"Parker!"

"Hey, monkey."

She puts her small hands on either side of his face and squishes his cheeks together until he looks like a damn fish. "I'm not a monkey."

He ruffles her hair before lifting her up and carrying her to the couch where he sits her on his lap and wraps his arms around her. He wishes he could shelter her from all of this. He wishes he didn't have to break her heart like he knows he's about to.

Bella giggles and tries to wiggle out of his arms. "You're being silly, Parker. I can't see the movie."

"Actually, princess, I need to tell you something. Can you listen for a minute and then, if you want, you can finish your movie with Dani?"

Bella nods and looks uncertainly from him to Dani and back again.

"Bella . . ."

Dani shifts closer to grab one of his hands and squeezes, letting him know she's there. Fuck, he really doesn't want to do this but knows he has to. So he takes a few breaths and tries again.

"Bell, something happened to Anne. She . . ." He takes another deep breath and starts again. "She was in an accident, princess."

"What kind of accident? Is she at the doctor's?"

"No, honey," Danielle says, placing a hand over the one he has holding Bella's.

"Bell, remember the story Anne told me about your parents when you were in the hospital?"

Bella nods. "She said that my mommy and daddy went to be with Jesus but they loved me very much."

"That's right, she did. Well, last night Anne went to be with your mommy and daddy, and Jesus."

Danielle squeezes his hand and when he glances at her, tears are streaming down her face, but she's trying to hide them. She's trying to be strong for Bella.

"My sister went to heaven?" Bella asks in a small voice.

"Yes, Bell."

Bella throws her arms tightly around his neck and cries

That night when he puts her to bed, Bella refuses to sleep with the light off.

"Is she asleep?" Danielle closes her book when he enters their bedroom.

"She finally fell asleep. She fought it." He pulls on a pair of pajama pants before crawling into bed beside her.

"I can't imagine what she's feeling right now. Losing her parents to a car accident two years ago and now her sister." She places the book back on the nightstand before switching off the lamp and moving closer to him.

"I just hope they let me adopt her. Bell's already been through a lot. I don't want to see her getting thrown into the system on top of everything else."

"Well, it's what Anne would've wanted." She snuggles up to him when she feels his arm settle around her shoulders. "She's tough though. No matter what happens, I think she'll be okay."

"I hope you're right, Dani."

A loud, ear-piercing screams erupts from the room next to theirs, and both Danielle and Parker rush out to Bella's room.

"Bell!" Parker gets to her room first but he's not prepared for the sight that greets him.

Bella's sitting up in her bed with her knees bent and she's breathing hard. Tears stain her cheeks and she's rocking back and forth with her arms wrapped around herself. Danielle rushes to her side and wraps her arms around her.

"Bell, did you have a nightmare?"

Bella unwraps her arms and clings to Danielle's shirt sleeve and nods her head yes.

"Do you want to talk about it?" she inquires, rubbing Bella's back, but Bella just shakes her head no.

"Do you want Danielle or I to stay in here with you?" Parker asks kneeling in front of her.

Bella shakes her head. "Can I sleep in your bed with you and Dani?"

He looks from Bella to Danielle and back again before standing and lifting Bella into his arms. "Come on, princess."

Danielle follows them back to their bedroom. Parker lays Bella down in the middle of the bed, covering her with the duvet. Dani climbs in, and Bella immediately snuggles up to her side and closes her eyes.

"Goodnight, princess." He leans over and kisses Bell's forehead before laying back down on his side of the king-sized bed.

Bella doesn't speak another word for the next couple days but she screams and cries every time Danielle or Parker leave her sight, even for a second.

Two days after the funeral Danielle and Parker get a call from the ministry letting them know they'll be sending someone out the next day to interview them and assess their ability to care for Bella.

CHAPTER TWENTY-EIGHT

"Mr. Collins?" The woman dressed in a black pantsuit, standing on the other side of their front door asks as soon as he opens the door.

"Yes."

"My name's Rebekah. I'm from the ministry. May I come in?" She holds her hand out for him to shake.

"Please." He takes a step back, opening the door wider, allowing her to come in. "Bella's playing outside with Danielle right now," he mentions over his shoulder as he leads her into the dining room.

"That's okay. I'd actually like to speak to you first." She lays her briefcase on the table and pulls out a folder.

"What would you like to know?"

"How long have you known Anne and Gabriella?"

"Anne and I grew up together, but we lost touch in high school. We reconnected again when she moved back here and took over guardianship of Bella."

"You're RCMP?"

"Yes, ma'am."

"In your file it says that you're a part of the ERT?"

"I am," he confirms,

"So, how will a six-year-old fit in with your busy schedule, Mr. Collins?"

"Our ERT only gets called in when we're needed on a case. Bella will be attending school full-time in September, and it won't be just me. Danielle will be taking care of Bella too."

"Danielle? Your girlfriend?"

A smile tugs at a corner of his mouth. "I'm hoping to make it more permanent than that soon."

Rebekah smiles knowingly then goes back to asking him more questions about how he intends to take care of Bella. She doesn't get a couple more questions in before the back door flies open with Bella running through it directly to Parker. Scrambling up his knees she puts her arms around his neck and cries, "Don't send me away, Parker."

He looks questionably at Danielle but she shrugs her shoulders. "We were going to go for a walk to the park, but she saw the strange car in the driveway."

Hearing her beg him not to send her away in that small voice breaks him, and the dam holding back his tears cracks until they're flowing down his cheeks.

"We're not sending you away, Bell," he says reassuringly, hopefully.

Bella peeks her face out from his neck and looks up at him. "You're not?"

"No, monkey. Danielle and I want you to live here now."

"If you'd like to," Danielle adds.

Bella lifts her head and nods enthusiastically while wiping at her tears. Her small hand moves to wipe away some of his tears too.

He knows in that instant this little girl will always hold a special place in his heart, no matter what the ministry decides.

Rebekah clears her throat and stands up, stuffing the folder back into her briefcase. "You should have an official decision in the mail in a few weeks, but I'm confident you have nothing to worry about. My visit today was just a technicality that has to be done for any case we receive to make sure it will be in the best interest of the child. But obviously Gabriella wants to stay here and I can tell that she'll be very much loved."

"I can stay?" Bella looks hopefully at Rebekah.

"Yes, you can stay."

Bella's mouth tips up into the biggest smile he's ever seen. After days of hearing her cry at night and watching her struggle with separation anxiety it's a relief to know she might finally be on the road to grieving and recovering from her sister's sudden death.

"Can I call you dad?"

Her question throws him off for a second, and he struggles with what to say. A part of him wants to say she can call him whatever she wants—a very big part of him, like ninety-nine percent of him. But that other one percent doesn't want to make promises he may not be able to keep. He doesn't want to say yes and get her hopes up only to have to crush them later on if the ministry decides against letting him adopt her.

Rebekah assures Danielle and Parker multiple times they'll be approved for the adoption of Bella, but a part of him doesn't want to believe it until they have the documentation in writing and in front of them.

He looks to Dani for a little direction, but she's just smiling at him through her tears and not really giving him much to help him decide how to answer Bella's question.

When he looks back at Bella there's a spark of hope in her eyes and he'll be damned if he'll be the one to crush that spark.

"You want me to be your dad?"

Bella doesn't say anything; she just nods her head.

He can't do it. He can't tell her no. Danielle was right about Bella having him wrapped around her finger. This little girl has been through too damn much in her six years. It will be his mission every day to make sure that spark stays in her eyes, and heaven help the fucker that ever tries to dull it.

"Bell, I want to be your dad too."

EPILOGUE

She could spend hours out here just sitting in the soft sand with her feet close enough the water hits her toes every time the waves crash on the shore, and the salty smell of the ocean with the cries of seagulls overhead. It's all so calming.

She's finally found her happy place, and as she glances over at Parker and Bella building the biggest sand castle they can, her heart warms. Here, with her man and her girl, is what life is all about.

It's the people you love and who love you back. It's not about the material things. It could all disappear tomorrow, but as long as she has the two of them and their friends she'll be okay.

The adoption papers went through last month and yesterday she and Parker got the documentation saying he was the official parent of Gabriella, or Bella. But neither of them needed documentation to tell them what they already knew.

She believes Bella claimed him as hers the first day they met. And Bella, well, Bella was always his. The two of them are like two peas in a pod. One never far away from the other. These two beautiful humans were her lobsters. She blames Kat and years of *Friends* reruns for that term.

Bella runs over to Danielle, giggling, and grabs a hold of both of her hands trying to pull her up.

"Come on, Mama."

"What are we doing?"

"Catching hermit crabs!" Bella calls over her shoulder as she runs back to join Parker.

The three of them are looking under various rocks along the beach and Bella has started chasing the crabs around in the sand when she stops suddenly next to Parker and peeks inside his hands.

"Dad caught one!" Bella yells to her.

Parker's on his knees in the sand with his hands clasped together, a wide grin on his face when she catches up to them. Bella's giggling and bouncing up and down on her toes next to him.

"Let's see it," Danielle tells him, trying to see in between the cracks of his fingers.

When he opens his hands there isn't a hermit crab inside of them. Instead, in its place is a small, black, velvet ring box.

He grabs her left hand as she gasps in shock, her right hand shooting up to cover her mouth.

"Yesterday we got the news we were parents to a beautiful six-year-old girl and now the only thing left is to make our little family official. Danielle Gilbert, would you do us the honor of marrying us?"

Looking from Parker to Bella and back again, she has no idea what to say. Her entire life she's felt liked she was worthless, like nobody in their right mind would ever love her. She can't believe that this past June was two years since she, Kat, and Alice moved to BC to get away from Adam and start new lives. And it's been six months since she met Parker and Bella in May. These two have proven her wrong, she wasn't worthless and there were people who loved her. Now, she finally feels like she's where she belongs. She feels like she's home.

"Say yes!" Bella tugs on the hem of her sweater.

"Yes!" Danielle laughs.

He slips the ring on her finger, then scoops her up and swings her around while Bella giggles next to them. "I love you."

"I love you both," she says, smiling down at Bella

THE END

PLAYLIST

"Wanted Dead or Alive" by Bon Jovi

"Girl Crush" by Little Big Town

"Dirty Laundry" by Carrie Underwood

"Scars" by Papa Roach

"In Too Deep" by Seventh Day Slumber

"Fucking Perfect" by P!nk

"Ain't Worth the Whiskey" by Cole Swindell

"Canadian Girls" by Dean Brody

"Drink A Beer" by Luke Bryan

"Bottoms up" by Brantley Gilbert

"Church Bells" by Carrie Underwood

"Over and Over" by Madeline Merlo

"Best Beers of Our Lives" by Chase Rice

"Just As I Am" by Brantley Gilbert

"Scars to Your Beautiful" by Alessia Cara

"Make me move" by Britney Spears

"I won't let you go" by Switchfoot

"Your Love is a Song" by Switchfoot

ABOUT THE AUTHOR

You can take the girl out of the ocean but you cannot take the ocean out of the girl. A.J. believes that describes her to a T. She practically grew up on a beach in Cape Town, South Africa until her family immigrated to Canada. However, the ocean still has a way of relaxing her. If she can't get to the water then a long drive with the music blaring will work just fine.

She wears her heart on her sleeve and is a self-proclaimed hopeless romantic who believes that everyone deserves their happily ever after. A.J. lives in BC, Canada with her husband. When she's not writing, she's reading. She loves the NFL and drinks way too much coffee.

If you enjoyed reading *Skin Deep* please leave a review on your favorite book retailer and/or Goodreads. Also, be sure to check out the sneak peek of *Piece of Me*, the second book in the stand alone series at the back of the book.

CONTACT HER:

EMAIL: a.daniels.author@gmail.com
FACEBOOK: A.J. Daniels Author
INSTAGRAM: A.J_daniels_author
TWITTER: AJDanielsAuthor

PIECE OF ME

PROLOGUE
Katherine

The thing about love is that you don't get to choose who you fall in love with or when you fall in love. Most of the time you never see it coming.

Then there are those times when you see it coming, and even though you try everything in your power to prevent it from happening it still smacks into you like a semi-truck. Just like the way I fell in love with Jason. He was my best friend. My protector. I was perfectly happy with our relationship the way it was.

As friends.

Until I wasn't.

I was about to learn that sometimes the person you don't want to love is the one you end up falling for the most.

And I fell hard.

CHAPTER ONE
Katherine

A loud, annoyingly obnoxious beeping rouses me from a very enticing dream. Hugh Jackman is doing really, *really* delicious things with his tongue and I don't want him to stop.

Damn, that man is talented.

When he lifts his head, I'm expecting that sexy Australian accent to do me in, but all that comes out when his lips move is the annoying beeping.

Frustrated, I throw my arm out in the general direction of my nightstand but instead of hitting solid wood, my arm connects with solid muscle and a huff sounds from my right.

The events of last night flash in my mind's eye like a stop motion movie. The six of us at the bar. Shots of tequila. *Lots* of tequila. Dancing by myself. Jay dancing with me. There was kissing. Lots of kissing, and lots of . . . touching.

I sit bolt upright suddenly realizing that I'm naked and the solid wall of muscle my arm just hit belongs to Jay.

Oh, fuck my life!

I run a hand down my face in horror. I can't believe I just slept with Jason. Sure, we've been flirting back and forth for over a year now but it was never meant to go beyond that. It was never meant to actually get physical. This is why I'm not allowed around tequila. It makes me do horribly stupid things that I'd never do when I'm sober.

I peek out of my right eye and am met by a set of very drool worthy abs.

Holy shit, the guy has the body of a Greek god.

A trail of golden hair leads down to that V muscle I love so much on guys. I'm slightly disappointed when the lower half of his body is covered by my navy blue duvet cover.

A slight chuckle snaps my attention away from that muscle and to his face. God, this man is sexy. Square jaw with light stubble, straight nose, and amazing, emerald eyes that are staring back at me. A smirk pulls at his lips. A lock of dark blond hair hangs down his forehead.

"Like what you see?" Jay teases.

I roll my eyes, "Don't look so pleased with yourself. Tequila was involved."

I gather the sheet closer around my body and move towards the bathroom.

Jay laughs. "You can keep denying it but this was bound to happen. And I wouldn't say no to another round . . . or two." He shoots me a wink when I poke my head out from the bathroom.

"Were you always this cocky?"

Jay grins. "Not cocky, babe. Confident."

I snort and roll my eyes turning back to start the shower, "Yeah, well, I'm confident this will never happen again," I call from the bathroom.

"You sure about that?" Jay says, startling me when he suddenly appears in the doorway.

"Seriously? Why do you have to sneak up on me like that." I grip the sheet tighter.

This man has the power to undo me and I'm not totally sure I'm okay with it. I like being in control, in all aspects. It was the reason for almost every one of my break ups and why I'm currently single. Men just don't like a woman who loves being in control.

But it was the one thing I didn't think I'd be able to give up. Being in control kept my anxiety at bay and I didn't like the way I felt when I was anxious.

I flake out of a lot of things when my anxiety runs rampant. I somehow manage to talk myself out of leaving my house and just staying curled up under my duvet watching Netflix. Even something as simple as going to the grocery store becomes a nightmare. I've quit many a job because of anxiety.

But this man standing in front of me, gloriously naked, is threatening to undo that control.

Jay cups my face with his hand and his thumb runs gently up and down my cheek bone, his emerald eyes staring intently into my amber ones.

"Stop fighting it," he whispers.

"I can't." I drop my head, causing his hand to fall away from my face.

I miss his touch instantly. I wish I was normal. I was I could just stay wrapped up in him. But I can't and I doubt I'll ever be able to.

Jay hangs his head and takes a step back. I want to reach out to him, to stop him from leaving, but my arms don't move and nothing comes out when I open my mouth.

"I'll see you around Kat."

I'm not sure how long I stand there staring out the doorway into my room. I don't even remember Jay getting dressed or hearing the front door open and close. But when I finally get into the shower the water is like ice.